Sek 4

Also by Onjali Q. Raúf

The Boy At the Back of the Class

The Star Outside My Window

The Night Bus Hero

The Lion Above the Door

The Great (Food) Bank Heist

Non-Fiction

Hope on the Horizon

Available in Audio Only

The Day We Met the Queen

ONJALI Q. RAÚF

The Boy at the Back of the Class

Illustrated by Pippa Curnick

Orion

ORION CHILDREN'S BOOKS

First published in Great Britain in 2018
by Hodder & Stoughton
This edition published in 2023

1 3 5 7 9 10 8 6 4 2

Text copyright © Onjali Q. Raúf, 2018
Illustrations copyright © Pippa Curnick, 2018

A CIP catalogue record for this book
is available from the British Library.

ISBN 978 1 51011 018 2

Printed and bound in Great Britain by Clays Ltd, Elcograf S.p.A.

The paper and board used in this book are made
from wood from responsible sources.

Dedicated to Raehan – the Baby of Calais.
And the millions of refugee children around the world
in need of a safe and loving home . . .

And to my mother and Zak. Always.

CONTENTS

THE EMPTY CHAIR

There used to be an empty chair at the back of my classroom. It wasn't a special chair. It was just empty because there was no one sitting in it. But then, one day just three weeks after school started, the most exciting thing that could ever happen to anyone, happened to me and my three best friends. And it all began with that chair.

Usually, the best thing about starting a brand-new term is that you get extra pocket money to buy new stationery with. Every year, on the last Sunday of the summer holidays, my mum takes me on an Extra-Special Adventure to hunt down my stationery set for the new school year. Sometimes I get so excited that my feet feel jumpy inside and I don't know which shop I want to go into first. There aren't many nice stationery shops where I live – they only ever have boring dinosaur sets for boys or princess sets for girls. So Mum takes me on the bus and train into the city where there are whole streets of shops – even huge department stores that look like tall blocks of flats from the outside.

Last year, I found a space-themed set with pictures of an astronaut floating past the moon. It was on sale too, so I bought a pencil case, a maths set, rubbers and a long ruler – and still had nearly a pound left over! The ruler is one of my favourite stationery pieces, because the astronaut floats across it in water mixed with silver stars. I played with it so much that the astronaut got stuck to one side and couldn't be bothered to move again. But it wasn't my fault. Mr Thompson, our teacher last year, had such a boring voice that my hands needed something to do. That's why it's important to have fun stationery with you in class – because you never know when you'll need to stop your brain from falling asleep or doing something that might get you into detention.

This year, I bought a Tintin and Snowy set. I love Tintin. Even though he's only a character in a comic book and isn't real, I want to be just like him when I grow up. I think being a reporter and getting to solve mysteries and go on adventures must be the best job in the world. My mum and dad used to buy me a brand new Tintin comic book for my birthdays, and Mum saves all the comics her library are about to throw away because they're too old or ripped and gives them to me, so I have a whole collection of them now. I've read them all at least fifty times. But I'll have to think of another pet to travel with because I'm allergic to dogs. I don't think cats or hamsters or even trained mice could be half as useful as Tintin's dog, Snowy. And even though I've thought about it for at least a year now, I still haven't come up with anything.

Because the Tintin stationery set was a lot more expensive than the astronaut one and wasn't on sale, I could only buy a pencil case, a small ruler and two rubbers. I had to think about it for a very long time but in the end, I decided spending all my pocket money in one go was worth it. Not just because everything had Tintin on it, but because if you press a button on the pencil case, Snowy barks and Captain Haddock's voice cries out 'Blistering barnacles!'. I've already been told off for pressing it in the middle of maths class this year, but if you can't press a barking dog button in maths then I don't see the point of it.

I don't like maths. Simple maths is fine, but this year we're learning about long division and square numbers and all sorts of things that my brain doesn't like doing. Sometimes I ask for help, but it's embarrassing putting your hand up too many times to ask the same question. I'm lucky because Tom and Josie and Michael always help me with the things I get stuck with. They're my best friends and we do everything together.

Tom's got short spiky hair and a side-smile and a big Adam's apple that looks like a ping-pong ball got stuck in his throat. He's the smallest in our group but he's also the funniest. He only joined our class last year after his parents moved here from America, but we became friends instantly. He has three older brothers who all tease and bully him. Not seriously – only for a joke. But I think they steal his food too which is why he's so skinny and always super-hungry. I once saw him eat a whole pizza with extra toppings and a double cheeseburger for lunch and still not be full up! So I hide my snacks and chocolate bars from him when I can.

Josie has large, brown eyes and at least a million freckles across her face. She's tall and gangly and is always chewing on her hair. She's the fastest girl in our year and can kick a football past any goalie from the other side of the pitch. She's the coolest person I know, and I've known her since we were three. Our mums say we became instant friends the first day we started nursery, so they decided to become friends too. I don't really remember much about myself at that age, but Josie is in all my school memories. We even got our first detention together last year – all because of a hamster called Herbert.

Josie had heard one of the upper school bullies say that he was going to flush our class hamster, Herbert, down the toilet at home-time. Josie told me, and we decided to go on a Hamster Rescue Mission. We hid Herbert in my rucksack before home-time and took him straight to my house. But of course, Mum found out and made me take him back the very next day. I tried to explain to boring Mr Thompson what had happened, but he wouldn't listen and gave me detention. And even though she didn't have to, Josie stood up and said she had helped to steal Herbert too – just so we could do detention together. You know a friend's a Best Friend when they're willing to sit in detention with you.

Michael has the neatest, puffiest Afro out of all the boys in our year. Most people think he's weird. But not us. His glasses are always broken, and his shoelaces are never done right, so he's always tripping up or bumping into things when he walks. But we're all so used to it now that we never notice. He's mostly quiet but when he does say something, grown-ups usually look impressed and say that it's 'ingenious' or 'insightful' or use other strange words beginning with 'in'. I don't know what they mean, but I guess they mean he's clever. Grown-ups always like coming up with long words for simple things.

Michael gets made fun of a lot because he can't run fast or kick a ball in a straight line, but he doesn't care. I wouldn't care either if I was as rich as him. His dad is a professor and his mum is a lawyer, and because they're always busy, they buy him all the latest gadgets and books and the coolest new games. When we went to his house last year for his birthday party, we saw his room for the first time. It looked like the inside of a toy store. I think it must be easier not to care about what people think when you've got that many toys in your life.

Josie and Michael are always competing with each other to see who can get the most gold stars and As in class. Michael is the best at history and Josie is the best at maths. But I'm better at reading and spelling than both of them – especially Josie. She hates reading and never, ever reads anything outside class. She says she doesn't have an imagination, so there's no point to reading books. I find that strange, because how can anyone not have an imagination? I think she must have had one when she was younger but that it was knocked out of her when she fell off her bike last summer. Mum says people without imaginations are dead inside. I don't think Josie is dead anywhere – she talks too much.

Having three best friends can make school seem like the best place to be, even on the most boring day. Although this year, school has become a whole lot more fun – and that's because of our new teacher, Mrs Khan.

Mrs Khan has extra bouncy hair and always smells of strawberry jam – which is much better than smelling of old socks like Mr Thompson used to do. She's new to the school and extra clever – much cleverer than Mr Thompson ever was. And she gives us prizes on Fridays when we've all been good. No other teacher in our year does that.

Mrs Khan lets us do all sorts of interesting things that we have never done before. In the first week of school, she helped us make musical instruments out of things we found in the school's recycling bin, and in the second week, she brought in a brand-new comic book to read to us that wasn't even in the school library yet.

Then in the third week, something happened that was so surprising and made everyone so curious, that even Mrs Khan couldn't make us focus on our lessons properly. And it all began with the empty chair.

It was on the third Tuesday after school had started, and Mrs Khan was taking the register. She was just about to call my name when there was a loud knock at the door. Usually when there's a knock on the door it's just someone from another class bringing a note, so no one really pays any attention; but this time it was Mrs Sanders, the Head. Mrs Sanders always wears her hair in the exact same way and peers over her glasses whenever she talks to anyone. Everyone is scared of her, because when she gives detention, she doesn't just make you sit in a room; she makes you memorise long words from the dictionary and doesn't let you leave until you've learnt them all off by heart – the meaning AND the spelling. I've even heard of lower graders being stuck in detention for hours because they had to learn words that were as long as this page!

So when we saw that it was Mrs Sanders at the door, we all fell silent. She looked very serious as she walked up to Mrs Khan, and we all wondered who was in trouble. After she had whispered and nodded for a few seconds, she suddenly turned around and, peering over her glasses at us, pointed to the empty chair at the back of the class.

All of us turned around to have a look at the empty chair. This was the chair:

As I said, it was a pretty ordinary chair, and it was empty because a girl called Dena left our class at the end of last year to move to Wales. No one really missed her except for her best friend Clarissa. Dena had been a bit of a show-off and was always talking about how many presents her parents got her every week and how many pairs of trainers she had and all sorts of other things that no one else cared about. She liked to sit at the back of the class because then she and Clarissa could pretend to be doing lessons when really they were drawing pictures of their favourite pop stars and giggling about someone they didn't like. Someone else could have taken the seat, but no one really wanted to sit next to Clarissa. That's why the chair had stayed empty.

After whispering for a few more seconds with Mrs Khan, Mrs Sanders left the classroom. We expected Mrs Khan to say something, but she seemed to be waiting, so we waited too. It was all very serious and exciting. But before we could start guessing about what was going on, Mrs Sanders came back, and this time she wasn't alone.

Standing behind her was a boy. A boy none of us had ever seen before. He had short dark hair and large eyes that hardly blinked and smooth pale skin.

'Everyone,' said Mrs Khan, as the boy went and stood next to her. 'This is Ahmet, and he'll be joining our class from today. He's just moved to London and is new to the school, so I hope you'll all do your very best to make him feel welcome.'

We all watched in silence as Mrs Sanders led him to

the empty chair. I felt sorry for him because I knew he wouldn't like sitting next to Clarissa very much. She still missed Dena, and everyone knew she hated boys – she says they're stupid and smell.

I think it must be one of the worst things in the world to be new to a place and have to sit with people you don't know. Especially people that stare and scowl at you like Clarissa was doing. I made a secret promise to myself right there and then that I would be friends with the new boy. I happened to have some lemon sherbets in my bag that morning and I thought I would try and give him one at break-time. And I would ask Josie and Tom and Michael if they would be his friends too.

After all, having four new friends would be much better than having none. Especially for a boy who looked as scared and as sad as the one now sitting at the back of our class.

THE BOY WITH THE LION EYES

For the rest of the day I kept sneaking glances over my shoulder at the new boy and noticed that everyone else was doing the same.

Most of the time he kept his head down low but every so often I'd catch him staring right back at us. He had the strangest coloured eyes I'd ever seen – like a bright ocean but on a half-sunny, half-cloudy day. They were grey and silvery-blue with specks of golden-brown. They reminded me of a programme I saw about lions once. The camera operator had zoomed into a lion's face so much that its eyes had taken up the whole screen. The new boy's eyes were like those lion's eyes. They made you want to never stop staring.

When Tom joined our class last year I had stared at him a lot too. I didn't mean to, but I kept imagining that he came from an American spy family – like the ones you see in the movies. He told me later that he had thought there was something wrong with me. The new boy probably thought there was something wrong with me too, but it's hard to stop staring at new people – especially when they have eyes like a lion's.

We had geography in first period that morning, so we couldn't get up to say hello to the new boy. Then at break-time I looked around the playground for him but couldn't see him anywhere. In second period we had P.E. but the new boy didn't join in; he sat in the corner staring at his rucksack, which was red with a black stripe on it and looked very dirty. I thought he must have forgotten his P.E. kit because his bag looked empty and saggy. I tried waving at him, but he never looked up – not even once.

Whenever we do P.E. I like to pretend that I'm training to join Tintin on an adventure, and have to be the super fastest human being on the planet. The only problem is my legs aren't as long as I want them to be yet, so even when I jump as hard I can, I always get stuck in the middle of the vault. Every birthday, I make a wish that I'll grow at least four inches taller, and I drink as much milk as I can so that my bones will stretch. But even though I'm nine and three-quarters now, I've only grown one-and-a-half inches since my last birthday. Or at least that's what my mum says. I tried my best to jump over the vault in one go in front of the new boy, but I got stuck again. Luckily, he didn't see me because he was staring at his rucksack the whole time.

After P.E. we had lunch-break, and Josie, Tom, Michael and me decided we would try and find the new boy so that he wasn't all on his own. We waited right next to the playground doors. But the new boy never came out. Tom even went to check the boys' toilets because that's where he had tried to hide on his first day when he didn't know anyone, but there was no one there.

'Maybe he's having lunch with the lower grades by mistake?' said Josie. But when we got into the lunch hall we couldn't see him anywhere.

In the afternoon we had history, and we were split into groups, but the new boy was allowed to sit on his own and not join in. Mrs Khan spent more time with him than she did with any of our groups, and she was pointing at things in a new workbook she had gotten him.

'Maybe he's deaf?' someone whispered.

'Maybe he can't speak English?' muttered someone else.

'There's definitely something wrong with him!' whispered everyone.

That afternoon I don't think any of us learnt about what it was like to be a gladiator living in Roman times, because we were all too busy whispering about the new boy. He must have known what we were doing because his face was red the whole time. Then, at last break, he disappeared again.

'He must be inside,' said Michael, after we had finished searching the whole playground for the third time in a row. By now, my lemon sherbets were getting sticky in my pocket and beginning to look like bright yellow fuzzballs.

At home-time, everyone was still talking about the new boy and wondering who he was. I think it was because a whole day had passed, and no one knew anything about him except for his name. Not even Clarissa – and she had been sitting right next to him!

People kept running up to her to ask if the new boy had said anything to her, but she just shook her head and said he was using a lower year workbook, so his reading and writing mustn't be very good.

On our way to the bus stop, we saw everyone crowding around Jennie just outside the front gates. Jennie is famous in school for always knowing something about everything, so we ran over to hear what she was saying.

Jennie is in the class next door and has the longest hair in school. She likes to spy on people and then tell stories about them to other people. Sometimes the stories are true, but most of the time they're only half-true because she makes things up. Last year she told a story about Josie cheating in a football match by pretending to fall down so she could get a penalty kick. But I was there and so was Tom, and we both saw her fall down after being kicked in the leg by an upper boy called Robert. She had a big fat bruise on her leg the shape of Australia for weeks afterwards! But no matter how many times we showed everyone the bruise and told them what really happened, no one believed us. Not even the people who were there.

Sometimes I think everyone likes to believe a lie even when they know it's a lie because it's more exciting than the truth. And they especially like to believe it if it's printed in a newspaper. I know that now. I also know why Mum says politicians are liars and always shouts at them whenever they come on the telly. Maybe Jennie will be a politician when she grows up.

When we got closer, we heard Jennie telling everyone that the new boy had spent all his break-times with Mrs Sanders because he had done something bad in his old school, and was too dangerous to be let out into the playground with us. But I didn't believe her; I could tell Michael didn't believe her either, because he asked her how she knew so much about it. Jennie got angry and crossed her heart and hoped to die that she had heard Mr Owen talking to Mrs Timms outside the teachers' staff room, and that both of them had said how sorry they felt for Mrs Khan and how glad they were that the new boy wasn't in their class because it wasn't going to be easy to deal with. But before we could ask her any more questions, Jennie's dad began to beep at her from his car, so she ran off.

We all watched her go and then looked back through

the school gates to see if the new boy had come out. But we couldn't see him anywhere.

'He's probably left already,' said Josie.

Tom and Michael nodded. 'Let's just wait two more minutes,' I said, hoping that he would still be inside. And I was glad I did, because a few seconds later, the new boy came out into the playground. He was holding Mrs Khan's hand and staring at the ground. A woman who was waiting by the outdoor benches suddenly shouted, 'Cooo-eeee!' and ran over to them. She was wearing a long brown coat, a woolly hat and a bright red scarf. She stood and talked to Mrs Khan for a long time and nodded an awful lot, but we couldn't hear anything because we were standing too far away.

'I wonder if that's his mum,' said Josie. I didn't think so because the new boy didn't hug her at all, and seemed shy around her too.

'Come on,' said Michael. He was pointing to his watch which was beeping like a submarine. Michael has a special watch that tells him when the next bus is coming. It's meant to help him get to places on time, but I've only ever seen it make him bump into things more quickly.

'No! Wait!' I said. And before I could think about it too much, I ran over to where the new boy was standing.

'Hello!' I said, tapping him on the shoulder.

Mrs Khan and the woman in the red scarf looked down at me as I reached into my pocket and got out the lemon sherbet. 'Here!' I said, holding it out. I was a little bit embarrassed because by now the sherbet was covered in fluff. But it was still good enough to eat. That's the good thing about lemon sherbets. No matter how bad they look, they still always taste delicious.

I think I must have spoken too loudly because the new boy took a step away from me as though he was frightened.

'It's all right, Ahmet, you can take it,' said the woman, motioning to him with her hands as if she was speaking in sign-language.

But the new boy grabbed her hand and hid his face behind her arm. I didn't know what to do because I've never really scared anyone so much before that they wanted to hide away from me. The woman spoke to him gently again, and after a few seconds he took the sherbet and looked straight at me with his lion eyes before hiding away again.

'Thank you,' said the woman. She looked at me and gave me smile. I liked her deep brown eyes because they seemed kind and her bright pink cheeks. But what I liked best of all was how her long blonde hair swirled around in the wind from underneath her hat. 'Ahmet will enjoy that on the ride home.'

I nodded and then ran back to where Josie and Tom and Michael were waiting for me. I felt extra happy because Mrs Khan had smiled at me with her whole face and had given me a wink too – just like my dad used to do whenever he thought I had done something good or when he was teasing my mum. When I'm a grown-up I'm going to wink at people just like he used to do and make them feel special too. And as we made our way home, I decided that the next day, whenever I saw the new boy staring at me, I was going to give him just as many winks as I could.

FORTY WINKS

The next day, and the next day and the next day after that, I smiled at the new boy and gave him a friendly wink, just as often as I could. My goal was to give him at least forty winks a day because that's what Mum says everyone needs, but after a while my eyebrows started to feel funny. I could tell the new boy was finding it interesting because he stopped looking at everyone else and kept looking at me. But then Michael saw me trying to wink with both my eyes, one after the other, and said I looked like I needed a doctor. He probably said that because I can't wink with my left eye as well as I can with my right eye. So I decided to stop winking quite as much.

That week Mrs Khan was teaching us all about photosynthesis and gave each of us a small pot with a seed in it to look after. Everyone was excited because she said there would be a prize for whoever grows the best plant. Even the new boy got one and I think it made him happy because he kept on looking at it. I tried to whisper lots of cheerful words like 'rainbow' and 'popcorn' and 'marshmallows' to mine, because I read somewhere that if you tell plants about happy things it makes them grow quicker. I'd never won a prize before. Not even at the fairground. I thought if I tried really hard and kept talking to my plant, I might win this time. And if I couldn't win then I wanted the new boy to, because he really seemed to like that plant.

But I was worried about Brendan-the-Bully-Brooker. He's the Class Bully. His cheeks are always pink because he spends most of his time chasing anyone smaller than him around the playground. He's not very clever and hates anyone that is. If anyone gets a top mark in class or a prize, he'll try and beat them up at home-time. I saw him looking at Ahmet's plant and narrowing his eyes, just like he always does when he's thinking of something mean to do. I didn't like it one bit.

His most common trick is to trip you up with his

foot. He also likes to tip up your lunch tray as he walks by so that your food dribbles down your chest like runny eggs. He's done that to me a few times. Sometimes he gets caught. But most of the time he doesn't. And even when he does get caught, he doesn't get detention.

Most of the teachers seem to like him though. Maybe it's because when he smiles, he looks like one of those boys that sing in a church choir on television. Mr Thompson used to call him 'a rascal' – which must be a good word because he gave Brendan-the-Bully a wink and a pat on the back whenever he said it, and then let him run off again. That made everyone else in class – except for Liam and Chris, Brendan-the-Bully's only two friends – hate him even more. Even the bullies in the upper years find him annoying. It's funny how bullies don't like other bullies. Maybe it stops them from feeling special. But in school everyone knows who the bullies are, and who they like to bully, and no two bullies can go after the same person. It's a strange system. But those are the rules and everyone sticks to them. Even the teachers.

But Mrs Khan is different.

She doesn't seem to like Brendan-the-Bully as much

as the other teachers. She's always watching him and ever since we were put in her class, he's been careful not to do anything around her. I'm still going to keep an eye on him though.

Soon after the new boy joined our class, lots of rumours about him began to be passed around the playground like an invisible game of pass-the-parcel.

Most people believed Jennie and said that the new boy must be dangerous and that's why he was never allowed out. But then other people started saying he had a super contagious disease, and that was the real reason why we weren't allowed to talk to him. The disease rumour scared Clarissa so much that she tried to sit as far away from him as she could without leaving her chair. One time she leaned over so far that she crashed right onto the floor! She didn't lean away so much after that, but she always put her arms up or used an exercise book as a divider.

I didn't think the new boy looked in the least bit dangerous or like he had an infectious disease, so the rumour I thought sounded the most true was the one that said he was from a super-rich family, and that his parents had sent him to our school under-cover so that he wouldn't be kidnapped. Michael said kidnappers wouldn't come to our school to look for him because it wasn't in a posh area and Tom agreed. He said that when he had moved from America, his older brothers had told him they must be poor now because they were going to live in the Poor End of London and not in the Rich End. I didn't really understand what he meant, because London doesn't have ends. On maps it just looks a spilt blob of jam.

I wanted to ask the new boy if the rumour about the kidnappers was true, and if he needed us to become his bodyguards. But he was still doing all his lessons on his own, and every break-time and lunch time he would disappear, so no one except for Clarissa could talk to him. And she didn't want to! I tried to catch his eye so I could smile at him and whisper 'hello', but Mrs Khan caught me and told me to pay attention to my work.

Next I tried to send him a note made into a paper plane – because I'm good at those – but it flew wonkily and hit Nigel on the head instead. He's a taddle-tale and told on me straight away. I hate taddle-tales because they seem to like getting people into trouble more than anything else in the world, and they always smile when they're doing it. Mrs Khan came and took the note and read it just to herself. She shook her head at me, but I think she must have found the drawing I made funny because her mouth gave a tiny smile that only I could see. Even though I didn't get told off, I knew it would be too risky to send any more messages by air mail. Especially with taddle-tales around.

The next day at break-time, Josie, Tom, Michael and I decided to follow the new boy and find out where he was going. But Mrs Khan caught us following him in the corridors and told us not to do it again. She didn't seem angry, but she did say that the new boy needed to be in 'Seclusion' for a little while longer, and that it was for his own good, so we promised not to follow him any more.

'What does "Seclusion" mean?' asked Josie when we went back out into the playground. None of us knew exactly, not even Michael, although he said it sounded as if the new boy needed to have private treatment like a really sick person in a hospital, so maybe he did have an infectious disease after all.

But it wasn't long until we found out what Seclusion really meant, and why the new boy needed so much of it.

WHAT MR BROWN AND MRS GRIMSBY SAID

My dad used to say that if you really, really want something, you have to keep on trying for it. And since he always used to say that he had everything he could ever want, I guessed he must have known all about trying for things.

I knew that I wanted to be friends with Ahmet. I didn't really know why, I just did. I gave up on trying to speak to him during the day – because of all the Seclusion he needed – but I figured after school was OK, because Mrs Khan had smiled at me and winked that first time. So every day for two whole weeks, I waited by the school gates at home-time.

As soon as the new boy and Mrs Khan came out to meet the woman in the red scarf, I would run over and give the new boy a lemon sherbet – and sometimes a whole chocolate bar. But no matter how many sweets I gave him or how much Mrs Khan encouraged him to talk to me, the new boy never said a word, and he never, ever smiled back. Not even when I gave him a whole packet of white mice, which are my favourite. He just quietly took the sweets and, staring at the floor, went and stood behind the woman in the red scarf as if he needed to hide from me.

'Maybe he doesn't like sweets,' said Michael, on the Friday of the second week.

'Don't be silly,' said Josie, chewing on her hair. 'Everyone likes sweets!'

'Maybe he's allergic?' said Tom. I'd never heard of anyone being allergic to chocolate and sweets before, but then again, I was allergic to dogs when no one else was. So maybe he was right.

After that, I decided to give the new boy my lunch fruit instead of my sweets. He was still going to his Seclusion every lunch-time, so on the Monday of the third week of trying to be his friend, I took the biggest orange I could find from the school canteen and waited by the gates. I was extra excited because I had drawn a smiley face on the skin, and Tom had given me a sticker of a dinosaur to stick on it – so that was two things that made the orange extra special. Tom loves collecting stickers – he has books and books of them at home and whenever he gets a new one he likes, he always brings it in to show us. I've never seen him give a sticker away to someone he doesn't know very well, so I hoped the new boy would like it and know how special it was.

But as we were waiting for the new boy to come out, we heard something about him that we didn't understand at all. In fact, it was even more confusing than learning about the Seclusion he was being given.

There were lots of grown-ups standing behind us at the gates – there always are at home-time. Sometimes, they talk about the news or what they're making for tea. But mostly they talk about the weather. I don't know why, because there's nothing more boring than talking about something everyone else can see for themselves, but I guess that's what you're meant to do when you become a grown-up.

Usually we don't listen because we have more interesting things to talk about, like what we're going to watch as soon as we get home and who our favourite Olympic athlete or footballer is. But this afternoon, just after someone had said how sunny it was and wasn't it lovely and how they hoped it would be sunny again tomorrow, someone else said, 'Have you heard about the new refugee kid that's joined the school? He's been put in Mrs Khan's class. They can't find an assistant that speaks his language. Poor little blighter!'

Josie and Michael and Tom all looked over at me and I looked back at them and then we stood very still together. I knew we were all thinking the exact same thing, because our faces frowned at the exact same time: we were wondering what a Refugee Kid was doing in our class.

Then the lady who had talked about the sun said, 'It'll cause trouble – you mark my words. They're only coming over to take our jobs!'

Carefully, so that no one else would see us, we all looked over our shoulders, and saw that it was Mr Brown and Mrs Grimsby who were talking.

Mr Brown shrugged and then said, 'If he's from that awful war on the news, I feel sorry for the kid. Can't blame 'em for wanting to get out of that death trap.'

'Hmph!' said Mrs Grimsby. 'A bother, the whole lot of 'em! Wouldn't trust one as far as I could throw 'em. Just you wait and see – it's our kids who will suffer, just because these ones are coming over to do whatever they like . . .' I could tell that Mr Brown didn't like what she was saying, because he frowned and shook his head and then took a step to the side.

I like Mr Brown. He's Charlie's dad. Charlie is one of the boys in upper school. Everyone knows who he is because he always steals at least three puddings from the pudding tray every lunch-time so there's never enough to go around. He's also famous for setting off the fire alarm to get out of a science test. He's always getting into trouble. But I don't think Mr Brown knows about that because whenever he cries out, 'Charlie my ol' boy! What have you been up to today?' and Charlie says 'nothing', Mr Brown beams at him. Charlie tells everyone that his dad is a boxer, but I don't think that can be true. He has a long beard, and if I was a boxer fighting him, I'd just pull his beard all the time and win.

I looked to the right over at Mrs Grimsby, her face all sour and pink and angry, and decided I didn't like her very much. She's the grandmother of a girl called Nelly who's in the year below us. Nelly's one of the most popular girls in school, mainly because she's won every burping competition the school's ever had. She can even burp-sing famous songs and is always challenging everyone to try and beat her.

32

I was looking up at Mrs Grimsby and thinking about all the things she had said when Josie suddenly poked me on the arm. 'Look!'

When I looked back through the railings, Mrs Khan and the new boy were in the playground and already talking to the woman with the red scarf. So I ran just as fast as I could and gave the new boy the special orange.

As usual, he didn't say thank you and he didn't smile, but I saw his eyes widen when he saw the drawing of the smiley face and the sticker on the orange. And for the first time ever, he looked up at me with his lion eyes and didn't look away. I knew right away that he wasn't frightened of me any more.

I stared back and gave a small smile. I wanted him to know that it didn't matter if he was a Refugee Kid. I still wanted to be his friend. I think he must have understood, because he gave me a nod that no one else could see. I wished he had smiled back, because you can only ever know that a person's really your friend when they like you enough to smile back at you. But it was OK because the nod felt like a promise, and I knew that I wouldn't have to wait too long before the smile followed.

THE REFUGEE KID

When I got home that night, I stayed up for as long as I could and waited for my mum to come back from work. It's always half past nine by the time she gets in on Mondays because Mondays are late-nights at the library. I'm supposed to be in bed by then or she gets cross, but I didn't mind being told off – not if it meant I could find out what had made the new boy a Refugee Kid and why Mrs Grimsby thought they caused trouble and took people's jobs all the time.

On the bus home, Michael said Refugee Kids came from big tents in the desert. But then Josie said that no one was allowed to live in tents in England except for when they were going on a camping trip, because it was against the law. And Tom said he'd heard of refugees on the television but couldn't remember why they were running away, and that England didn't have any deserts with lots of tents in it anyway. It was all very confusing, but I knew my mum would know because she works in a library, and libraries have books about everything.

My mum is amazing and the most cleverest person I know – even cleverer than Mrs Khan. She works two jobs – she's a librarian during the week and on Saturdays, she's a carer. She looks after people who can't eat or walk or remember things properly any more or who are too sick to live on their own. Because Mum has to work all the time, I don't get to see her lots – except on Sundays. Sundays are our special Adventure Days – we used to have them all the time with my dad. Whenever he had a day off, he would wake us up early, pack a lunch and we'd set off in the car for an adventure! Usually to the seaside or a safari park, or, if the weather was cold, for bowling or a movie.

We can't really afford to do any of those things now, because when I was six years old, my dad died in a car crash. Sometimes I worry that I'm forgetting him, even though I miss him every day. But when I think hard and dive right down into the deepest part of my brain, he's still there. He was the funniest dad anyone could ever have. He used to be a carpenter and loved to build things out of whatever he could find.

This is what Dad looks like in my memory:

He always talked a lot more than Mum and loved to make up stories. But more than anything, he loved listening to music. He had a huge music collection, and he was always fixing the old-fashioned record player my grandfather had bought for him for his thirteenth birthday. He taught me how to play the big black discs on it and how to polish the large golden sound horn properly.

Mum was going to sell it last year to help pay the bills – because apparently the older something is the more money it's worth. Only for things, that is – not people. But luckily my Uncle Lenny made her give it to me instead. Uncle Lenny's my mum's brother and is the best uncle in the world even though he's married to my Aunt Christina who I don't really like, and has a son called Jacob who likes breaking things. He tries to visit us at least once a week, usually on his own. He's always asking me if there's anything I need. I love that about him. And I'll always love him for helping me keep Dad's record player. It's in my room now, but I never play music on it unless Mum is out of the house. She doesn't like me using it very much. I think it reminds her of when my dad used to dance around with her after he'd made a chair or table he was proud of, and it makes her too sad.

I had been playing one of my dad's favourite old records to stop myself from falling asleep, when I suddenly heard my mum's key in the door. You can always tell when it's her key in the door and not my

Uncle Lenny's, because it jangles the loudest. I quickly turned the song off and ran to the living room.

'Well, hello there, munchkin!' said Mum. I could tell she was surprised to see me because her eyebrows had jumped up and disappeared into her hair. 'What are you doing up so late?'

'I can't sleep,' I said.

'Ah!' she said. Giving me a hug, she looked at me with a frown and touched my forehead. She always touches my forehead when she's worried about me.

'You're not feeling ill, are you?'

I shook my head.

'Have you had your supper?'

I nodded. I usually have a tin of soup and a bread roll for supper on the nights Mum can't make it home in time for dinner. Mrs Abbey from next door comes and helps me make it when she knows I'm going to be on my own. She's old and has trouble walking, but sometimes she makes me fish fingers if she's feeling well. My favourite soup is tomato soup because it reminds me of tomato ketchup. Ketchup is one of my most favourite things to eat in the whole wide world. You can add a dollop of ketchup to any dish that's not a dessert, and I'll bet you my pocket money it'll make that dish taste instantly better! It's third on my list of top foods, after chocolate and ice cream that comes in a cone from an ice-cream van.

'Well then,' said Mum, as she put her bags down. 'Let's see if a little hot chocolate doesn't put you to rights! Come and keep me company while I have some tea. I'm not that hungry today.'

I followed Mum into the kitchen and watched her get out the cocoa jar and switch on the kettle. And then before I knew it, I asked, 'Mum, what's a Refugee Kid?'

I didn't really mean to blurt it out like that, but sometimes my mouth does things my brain isn't ready for.

Mum stopped what she was doing and stared at me.

'A *refugee kid*?' she asked, with a frown on her face. 'Where did you hear those words?'

'At school,' I said. 'Someone called the new boy in our class a Refugee Kid.'

'You've got a new boy in your class?'

I nodded.

'And Mrs Khan didn't tell you anything about him?'

I shook my head. 'Only that he's called Ahmet and he's never been to London before. I've been trying to make friends with him, but he doesn't talk to anyone so I can't tell if he wants to be friends back . . .'

'I see . . .' Mum fell silent. She poured the milk into the milk pan, and waited for it to heat up. I knew she was thinking about something serious, because she was rubbing her chin a lot. Mum only ever rubs her chin when she is about to say something serious.

'Mum?' I whispered.

But Mum stayed silent which made me start to worry. Mum usually answers my questions right away. Maybe what Mr Brown had called the new boy wasn't a nice thing to call him at all.

While I waited for my hot chocolate, I went and sat down in my chair and looked out of the window. Our flat isn't very big but we have a small table near the window with four chairs around it. I always sit in the chair next to the fridge because I like being able to open the fridge door without getting up. It's like looking into an extra room in the house – but one that's filled with food instead.

Whenever I go to my Uncle Lenny's house I always

look in his fridge, because his one is so big it almost touches the kitchen ceiling. If he had to, my Uncle Lenny could live in his fridge. He'd have to take out all the shelves and things, but he could definitely live in it standing up if he wanted to. I think it's good to have a fridge that's big enough to stand in. It means you'll never run out of food like we do sometimes. And if you do, you can go and have a wonder in it.

When Mum had finished making the hot chocolate and her tea, she sat down in her chair which is opposite mine, and took out two lumps of sugar from the sugar jar. Keeping them balanced on a spoon, she slowly swirled them into the tea in little circles. We both watched them get smaller and smaller until they disappeared.

'Mum . . . can you tell me then? What's a Refugee Kid – I mean, where do they come from?'

Mum gave me a look. She has at least twenty different looks that give me a secret message, and I know what all of them mean. This one meant, *stop asking me*. Then she said, 'Do you remember those lifeboats on the telly, darling? The ones with lots of people squeezed in that you were asking about?'

I nodded. It had been in the middle of the summer holidays. Mum and I were in the sitting room. She was doing a crossword and I had been colouring in some drawings I had done, and the news was on in the background. The TV screen had suddenly changed from a woman reporter standing on a beach to a video of lots of people in boats in the middle of an ocean, all looking scared. I had felt sorry for them and asked Mum what was going on.

'Do you remember what I said?' asked Mum.

'You said . . . that they were trying to find somewhere new to live because their home wasn't nice to live in any more.'

'Exactly, my love. They were what people call *refugees*. And children like the new boy in your class are called refugee kids, because they've had to leave their homes, and travel very far to try and find a new house to live in.'

'Do you mean like Dena?' I asked, wondering if Dena was going to be called a Refugee Kid in her new school too. She had to move to Wales because her mum and dad couldn't find a house in London.

Mum shook her head. 'Not exactly,' she said. 'Dena's mum and dad *wanted* to move. They had a choice, and they wanted to live in a much bigger, nicer house than the one they already had. But refugee children have been *forced* to run away – because bad people have made it impossible for them to stay. Those bad people drop bombs on their houses and destroy all the beautiful parts of their cities. And the places where the refugees used to live have become so horrible and so scary that they can't live in them any more. So they walk for miles and miles and get into boats to travel to countries they've never been to before, and go to strange places they don't know, just so they can find somewhere that's safe enough to live in again.'

'Oh,' I said quietly. I wondered what the refugees had done to make the bad people so angry. Last year, two first graders in school had tripped over Brendan-the-Bully to get back at him for chasing them, which made him so angry that he smashed open their lunch boxes and stomped on all their food.

'What did the refugees do to make the bad people want to hurt them?' I asked, thinking it must have been something very bad to make someone want to drop a bomb on their houses.

Mum shook her head. 'Nothing at all, darling. The bad people are just much stronger than they are, and like to feel big and powerful by bullying them. You see, some people think that by taking things away from other people and hurting them, it gives them more power. And the more power they have, the more they want, and the greedier they get. So they go on hurting more and more people until everyone wants to run away.'

'Just like the bullies at school!' I said, feeling angry.

'Well . . . I guess it is sort of like that,' smiled Mum. 'Except the bullies the refugees are running away from are a lot bigger and far more horrible. They force people to leave everything they ever had behind. Even the people they love most in the world.'

I thought about the new boy and felt sorry for him. Maybe he had been forced to leave behind lots of things that he loved most in the world, and that's why he didn't talk to anyone and needed so much Seclusion. I tried to think of what I would leave behind if I had to run away from lots of bullies. But I couldn't decide. All I know is that I could never leave my dad's record player behind – or his favourite hammer, which is still in the bottom kitchen drawer.

Mum got up and took her mug to the sink. 'Now, I know you want to make friends with this new boy, but you mustn't be too eager. He'll need lots of time and space first. OK?'

I nodded, even though I didn't really understand what she meant. If I was the new boy, I would use up all my time to make as many friends as I could – especially if I had just run away from bullies that were bigger and more horrible than the bullies at school! I wondered if I should tell my mum about all the lemon sherbets and white mice and the orange with the smiley face I had given him, but then she said, 'The world has never been kind to refugees,' in a sad way. She sounded just like she did whenever she talked about my dad. So even though I wanted to ask at least four more questions, I decided not to say anything else.

'Now drink up and off to bed! And I'll come and tuck you in, in just a few minutes.' Mum came and ruffled my hair. She always ruffles my hair when she wants me to think she's happier than she really is.

I drank the rest of my hot chocolate just as quickly

as I could and ran to bed. Mum only ever tucks me into bed when she's home early, so this was a special treat. I love being tucked into bed – even more than I love beating everyone else in a race or scoring a goal. It's the best feeling in the world to be wrapped up all warm and fuzzy in a blanket by someone you love more than anyone else on the planet, and who loves you right back.

As I lay waiting for Mum to come in, I thought about all the things she had said – about the bombs and the boats and the bad people who were so greedy that they made everyone want to run away from them. I had so much to tell Josie and Tom and Michael! Especially as I don't think their mums and dads would have told them half as much as my mum had told me.

It's one of the things I love most about Mum. She always tries to answer my questions no matter how tired she is or how hard my questions are. And she always tells me the absolute truth. Michael's parents are always saying 'Not now dear' or 'We'll tell you when you're older', and Josie's mum keeps telling her that girls are meant to be quiet and not to ask so many questions. But my mum never says anything like that to me. I think it's because of all the books she reads. Mum says that the best books leave you with more questions than answers, and that that's the fun part – you have to try and find the answers for yourself somewhere else. And Dad used to say that the more questions you ask, the more clever you'll be. Because that's the only way you'll ever know more than you already do.

I think this is the first time in my life that I've ever wanted to be extra, *extra* clever about anything, because by the time Mum had come to tuck me in for the night, I had a long list of questions in my head that I wanted to ask the new boy. Eleven exactly. This is what they looked like:

My 11 Questions
  1. Where did you have to run away from?
  2. What language do you speak?
  3. Who's the woman in the red scarf?
  4. Do you have any brothers or sisters?
  5. What did the bullies do to make you run away?
  6. Did you have to get on a boat like the people on the news?

7. What sports do you like best?
8. What's your favourite fruit?
9. How far did you have to walk to get away from the bullies?
10. Do you like it here or do you miss your old house more?
11. Do you have a best friend?

My eleven questions would help me know everything I needed to know about the new boy so that I could be his friend. And I was going to find out the answer to every single one of them.

THE WOMAN IN THE SILVER SCARF

As soon as I got to the bus stop the next day, I told Josie and Tom and Michael everything my mum had told me about Refugee Kids, and about how the new boy had probably had to get on a boat with no toilets on it so that he could run away from bombs and all the other bad things that the bullies had done to his country.

'But my dad said Refugee Kids are dangerous, and that they lie and steal things,' said Josie, looking confused. 'He told me to stay away from the new boy and not to talk to him, because he was probably a criminal!'

'But *my* mum and dad said we should be extra nice to him. Look!' And opening up his rucksack, Tom showed us a big bag of sweets. 'Mum said to give these to him at lunch-time. *And* she said we had to be nice to him and not to ask him too many questions.'

'My mum said the same,' said Michael as we got on the bus to school. 'Except she told me to give him a banana. And my dad said Refugee Kids were running away from the war that's on the television all the time. He didn't say anything about any bullies!'

We all looked over at Josie, who was chewing on the ends of her hair and frowning. She didn't say anything, but I knew she was thinking that her dad must have made a mistake. There was no way the new boy could be dangerous or a criminal – not when he was the same size as us and had just run away from bullies and a real war.

Mr Thompson had taught us all about wars last year. It had been a special year for wars and Mrs Sanders said it was our duty not to forget about them. We learned about red poppies and how they were the most important flower because they grew on soldiers' graves, and about how lots of countries had joined up to fight in the very first war. The upper years did an assembly about it and we went on a special day trip to the Tower of London where the Queen keeps her crown, because that's where millions of red poppies had been put in its gardens and stuck on its walls.

Mr Thompson said we should never forget how many people have died in wars to save us, but I can't remember long numbers, especially ones that keep going up all the time. But I'll never forget that castle. It had looked like it was bleeding. And later on that day, a man who knew all about the first big war gave us an extra-special lesson inside the castle. His name was Officer Denny. I remember him because his name rhymed with my Uncle Lenny's.

Everyone liked him because he was funny and knew everything there was to know about bombs and uniforms and a sad place called Flanders Field. He picked me and Michael to try and hold up a rucksack that was the same size and weight as a real soldier's rucksack. But it was so big and heavy that we couldn't even lift it up off the ground!

Remembering Officer Denny's rucksack made me wonder if the new boy had to carry lots of heavy things in his rucksack when he was running away. Maybe that's why it looked so old and dusty. He still didn't have a new one – but that week he had started to wear the school uniform. He must have found the new shirt and jumper itchy because he kept pulling at the collar whenever he thought no one was looking.

That day the bus to school was late and got stuck in so much traffic that the driver let everyone get off early. We had to run half the way and by the time we got to the playground, the bell had started ringing. I was hot and sweaty and feeling icky when we got into class, so I didn't realise that everyone was quieter than usual. But after a few minutes, I noticed that Parvinder and Dean – who were clever at everything and sat at the front of the class – kept looking over their shoulders. At first, I thought they were looking at me because my face was still red, but then I heard Parvinder say, 'Wonder who she is!'

I turned around and saw a grown-up sitting in Clarissa's seat. And not just any old grown-up, but one who was talking to the new boy! And the new boy was talking back to her!

I poked Josie in the arm and said, 'Look!'

Josie turned around and whispered, 'Where's Clarissa?'

We looked around the classroom and then saw that Clarissa was sitting at the end of our row on Felicity and Natasha's table. She looked much happier.

'Hurry up and settle down please!' said Mrs Khan, as she picked up the register. 'Before we head to assembly, I want to introduce someone very special to you. But let's make sure you're all here first!'

After she had finished calling everyone's names, Mrs Khan said, 'Now class, I want you all to say good morning to Ms Hemsi, our new class assistant.'

Ms Hemsi stood up and smiled at everyone.

'Good moor-ning, Ms Hemseeeeeeeee!' we all said. Half the class shouted it out, and the other half said it quietly – as if they weren't sure Mrs Khan had given them the right name to say. I shouted it out. I like shouting out new names. It makes them feel more real.

Ms Hemsi smiled and said, 'Good morning, everyone!'

'Ms Hemsi will be helping Ahmet with his lessons from now on. If we're very lucky, in a few weeks, she will be helping Ahmet do a presentation about his home town, and how he feels about being here in London.'

Everyone turned to stare at Ms Hemsi as she nodded and smiled and then sat back down.

'She looks nice,' whispered Josie. 'I like her scarf!'

I looked back over my shoulder because I liked the scarf Ms Hemsi was wearing on her head too. It looked like a silver river and it had a diamond pin clipped on to one of the sides that looked like a star. She had one of those smiles where the person smiling never shows any teeth, but I liked it. And her eyes looked like they'd been drawn around with thick black pencil which made them look bigger and more interesting.

The new boy seemed to like her too and when she sat back down, she whispered something to him and patted him on the back which made him nod. I felt happy for him. He had someone to talk to, and he didn't have to sit next to Clarissa any more. It's much nicer to sit next to someone who isn't always trying to get away from you all the time and has a diamond pin in her scarf.

All that day, the new boy did his lessons at the back of the class, and at break-time and lunch-time he went to Seclusion as usual. But, maybe because Ms Hemsi was with him, he didn't look at the ground so much and seemed more interested in everything we were doing. I caught him staring at me and Josie twice before lunch-time and three whole times in the afternoon, and I was sure he wanted to be friends with us now.

At home-time, we waited just as we always did by the gates – but this time, all of us had something to give him. Josie had saved her chocolate yoghurt pudding from her lunch box for him especially, and Michael and Tom had the bag of sweets and the banana their mums and dads had told them to save. Today I had an apple to give him – because the school canteen had run out of oranges. But it was OK, because Tom had given me a sticker of a whale to put on it, so it was still special.

As we were waiting, I crossed my fingers and secretly hoped that Ms Hemsi would come out with the new boy too, because since she could speak to him properly, she would be able to ask him some of my eleven questions.

The playground had started to empty by the time the new boy finally came out, holding both Ms Hemsi's and Mrs Khan's hands. As they made their way over to the woman in the red scarf, Michael whispered, 'Come on!' I could tell he was excited because his eyes had gotten wider. Michael's eyes always get wider when he can't wait to do something.

We all ran over to the new boy and gave him our gifts.

'This is from me,' said Tom, holding out the large bag of sweets like it was a trophy. 'There are cola bottles in there – and flying whizbees and some toffee melts too!'

'And this is from me,' said Josie, holding out the chocolate pudding. 'It's my favourite!'

'Er . . . this is just a banana. But look!' said Michael, turning it over to show the new boy the row of stick men he had drawn on it.

'And this is from me,' I said, holding out the apple.

The new boy looked up, his arms full, and gave us each a happy nod. I could tell it was a happy nod and not just an ordinary nod because even though his mouth wasn't smiling, his lion eyes looked happy.

Ms Hemsi bent down and said something in a foreign language into the new boy's ears. He nodded and then, looking up at us, said very slowly, 'Thank . . . you . . . friends.'

Josie, Michael, Tom and me nodded and beamed, and then, all at once, started talking.

'Do you want to come play football with us tomorrow?' shouted Tom. 'At break-time?'

'I'll get you another one of those puddings tomorrow if you like them!' exclaimed Josie.

'I'll ask Mum to give me something better than a banana!' cried out Michael. 'What about some mini muffins?'

'And I'm going to get something better than an apple tomorrow! What's your favourite fruit?' I asked.

The new boy looked at us and then looked up at Ms Hemsi and Mrs Khan and then at the woman in the red scarf. They were all smiling and the woman in the red scarf ruffled his hair just like my mum had ruffled my hair the night before.

'Now, kids,' said Mrs Khan, bending down so that her face was the same height as ours. 'These are all wonderful gifts. And I know Ahmet is thankful for them. But he needs to learn just a little bit more English before he can answer your questions, OK?'

We all looked at each other, and then at Mrs Khan, and then nodded.

'But I do think that's a very good idea of yours, Tom. Maybe Ahmet *would* like to play football with you tomorrow at break-time!' Ms Khan looked over at Ms Hemsi, who gave a nod. 'Yes, that's a very good idea.'

'Awesome!' said Tom, and he was so excited that he gave the new boy a thump on the arm. The new boy looked at Tom and then at his arm as if he wasn't quite sure what had just happened.

'And there's no need to give him so many presents every day,' said the woman in the red scarf, laughing. 'It's so lovely, but we don't want to rot Ahmet's teeth now do we?'

We all shook our heads.

'If you still want to give him something at home-time, just choose one thing between you all and that'll be more than enough. OK?'

We all nodded, and then I cried out, 'Ms Hemsi!' I hadn't meant to say it so loudly, but I was so excited at the thought of having one of my questions answered that I couldn't help myself.

'Yes?' smiled Ms Hemsi.

'Can I ... er ... where is he from? Like, which country? And what language does he speak?' I asked, looking at the new boy.

Ms Hemsi's smile widened – even though she still didn't show any of her teeth. 'Ahmet is from a country called Syria, and he speaks a language called Kurdish.'

'Do you speak that AND English?' asked Josie, looking impressed.

'Yes,' said Ms Hemsi. 'I'm Syrian too.'

'Why doesn't Ahmet speak any English?' asked Tom.

'Well . . .' said Ms Hemsi. 'Because in Syria nobody needs to speak English. Just like you don't need to speak a Syrian language here in England.'

'Oh.' The answer made Tom frown to himself, which meant he was asking himself lots of other questions in his head.

'Now, kids, off you go,' said Mrs Khan, clapping her hands. 'Ahmet needs to get going and so do you. And Tom – I notice you're wearing your brother's trainers by mistake again! Try and make it the last time, OK?'

'Yes, Miss,' said Tom, as he turned bright red.

We waved goodbye and headed to our bus stop. Just before we turned the corner, I looked over my shoulder and saw the new boy take a big bite of the apple I had given him. I felt even happier than I did when Ms Hemsi had answered my questions! But a second later the feeling quickly disappeared, because that was when I saw Brendan-the-Bully.

He was standing in front of the boys' toilets just a few yards away, and his cheeks were pink and his eyes were narrow, and he was watching the new boy with a scowl on his face. Everyone knows that Brendan-the-Bully hates anyone who's different from him, but it was the first time I had seen him look so angry and mean. He couldn't do anything because Ms Hemsi and Mrs Khan and the lady in the red scarf were there, but as we headed to our bus stop and all the way home, I couldn't help feeling worried. I think I knew right away that the scowl was a warning, and that he was going to make things hard for the new boy and anyone who wanted to be friends with him.

And it turns out that I was right. Because at first break on the very next day, that's exactly what he started doing.

MR IRONS' NOSE

When the bell rung for first break the next morning, Mrs Khan kept her promise and let the new boy out into the playground for the very first time. Tom was put in charge of looking after him and we were all told that if he got scared or wanted to stop playing, then we were to find a teacher immediately or go and see Ms Hemsi in the staff room. I didn't know why the new boy would be scared of being in the playground, or why he wouldn't want to play with us, but then I thought that maybe in his country, the bullies had been mean to him at school too. I'd never really thought about it before, but maybe there are bullies in everyone's playground.

As Josie grabbed her football, Tom tried to explain to the new boy how to play the game properly.

'YOU! Like THIS!' said Tom loudly, pointing to the new boy, then his foot and then the ball. The new boy nodded.

'But NOT like THIS!' continued Tom, shaking his head before pointing to the football and then his hand.

'This is stupid! He *knows* how to play football!' said Michael.

'Maybe they play it differently in his country. Remember when I got here and I only knew American football?' protested Tom, looking at me as if I knew the answer.

I shrugged. 'I don't know! We should have asked Ms Hemsi!'

'Oh, come *on*!' cried Josie as we reached the playground. 'Let's just let him try and see if he knows it.'

By the time we had reached our usual corner of the playground, Josie and Tom had decided that the new boy would be on Josie and Michael's team. Since she was the best at football, it wouldn't matter so much if the new boy couldn't play. And because it was just Tom and me on my team, we had the first kick.

After less than a minute of the game starting, the new boy began to run and dribble and do lots of tricks with the football that none of us could do yet. And within the first five minutes, he had scored two goals.

'Whoah!' said Tom. 'He's even better than Josie!' Suddenly catching Josie's eye, he quickly added, 'Or nearly as good, anyway!'

'Wooooohooooooo!' cried out Michael as the new boy flashed past me and Tom and struck another goal. 'Wooooohoooooo!'

By now, a crowd was beginning to gather to watch the game, and I could hear lots of upper graders and lower graders talking and saying things like, 'Look! The dangerous kid's been allowed out!' and 'Does this mean he doesn't have a disease?' and 'But the kidnappers will be able to see him from here!'

I had just heard Jennie tell everyone that she was sure she had heard Mrs Sanders say the new boy was a professional footballer, when she suddenly cried out 'OOOOWWWWW!' and before we knew what was happening, Brendan-the-Bully and his mates, Liam and Chris, had pushed their way onto our make-believe pitch.

Josie looked at me and I looked at Tom, and Tom looked over at the new boy, who was standing next to Michael looking confused.

'We want to play,' said Brendan-the-Bully, a nasty smile on his face. He walked over to the new boy, who had the football, and kicked the ball away so hard that it ended up on the other side of the playground. The new boy took a step back.

'Go away, Brendan,' said Josie, bravely. 'This is our game and that's MY ball!'

Brendan-the-Bully turned around to look at Josie, and she swallowed nervously. But just then his expression changed from mean to sad.

I turned around too and saw that Mr Irons was walking towards us.

'What's going on here then?' he asked, his moustache twitching.

Mr Irons is one of the upper school teachers and is famous for being one of the strictest teachers in school and for never, ever smiling. He has a long face, a long nose, long lips and a large brown bristly moustache that he carries a tiny comb for in the front pocket of his jacket. Everyone knows about the comb, because when he thinks no one is looking he takes it out and combs his moustache with it in short, straight lines. And when he gets very angry you can hear his nose whistling. If that happens, then you know you're going to get at least one detention or be given a hundred lines to write.

He's also the very worst teacher you can have on break-duty because he hates noises – especially happy noises. Whenever he's in the playground, he walks around telling everyone off for laughing too loudly or for making fun sounds. Last year he made a first-year boy who was playing 'tag' cry by telling him that only pigs squeal, and since the boy was squealing, he must come from a large family of pigs and should spend the rest of break inside. And another time, Mr Irons gave everyone cheering for Handstand Hannah a hundred lines to write for being so loud – even though she was about to beat the world record for the Longest Handstand in History!

Whenever anyone sees Mr Irons walking towards them, they always play more quietly or move away. But we had been so happy that the new boy was playing with us that we had forgotten we were in a school where there were bully bullies and teacher bullies!

'Please, Sir,' wailed Brendan-the-Bully. 'She won't let me play! I wanted to play, and she said I couldn't!'

Mr Irons tutted at Josie. 'That's not a very nice thing to do to your friend, is it?'

'He's not my friend!' said Josie angrily. 'And he didn't ask! He came over and kicked our ball away!'

'Please, Sir, and that boy over there told me I couldn't play too!' added Brendan-the-Bully, pointing at the new boy and smirking.

Mr Irons looked over at the new boy and then beckoned for him to come over. The new boy looked around, and then, realising what he was being asked to do, walked over to where Mr Irons was standing.

'Did you tell this boy he couldn't play with you?' asked Mr Irons, pointing to Brendan-the-Bully.

The new boy looked around again. Everyone else in the playground had stopped what they were doing and were listening to everything that was being said.

'Please, Sir! Brendan's lying,' I cried out, running up behind the new boy.

'Yeah!' added Michael.

'And he's new,' I added. 'And he doesn't spea—'

'When I WANT your opinion, I'll ask for it! But until then, DON'T interrupt me again!' shouted Mr Irons. I felt my whole face go red and my tongue swell up in my mouth. I could see Brendan-the-Bully smirking again, but this time at me.

66

'Now, *boy*.' Mr Irons turned to the new boy. 'I'll ask you again! Did you, or did you NOT, tell Brendan he couldn't play with you?'

The new boy stood rooted to the spot and looked over at us.

'But, Sir!' I burst out. 'You don't understand! He can't spea—'

'RIGHT!' shouted Mr Irons, his nose whistling dangerously. 'That's detention for you!' he cried out, pointing to me. 'And you!' he added, pointing to the new boy. 'And you!' he hissed out, pointing to Michael. 'All three of you, come see me after school today. Until then, I'm confiscating this ball!'

Josie watched angrily as Liam handed the ball to Mr Irons with a grin.

As we watched Mr Irons walk off with the ball under his arm, the bell rang for the end of break. Brendan-the-Bully smiled at us.

'See you at lunch, then!' he said, and ran off.

But at lunch-time the new boy was nowhere to be seen, and at second break, Ms Hemsi came out with him, so Brendan-the-Bully stayed away from us. At home-time, Tom had to run off to catch the bus because it was one of his brothers' birthdays. The rest of us decided that, instead of going to see Mr Irons, we would go and find Mrs Khan to see if she could help us. Even though Ms Hemsi had already spoken to her about what had happened, we also knew that she didn't know the whole story because Ms Hemsi hadn't been there. So telling the new boy to follow us, we went and spoke to Mrs Khan.

She listened to us in silence and then, when we were finished, she shook her head. 'Ridiculous,' she muttered, and I think she was talking to herself. 'Some people just can't see past the end of their own noses!' She looked up at us and smiled. 'Not to worry! All of you come with me!'

As we walked to the other side of the school to reach Mr Irons' classroom, I thought about what Mrs Khan had said about noses and their ends. I touched my own nose and squashed it down, because I didn't ever want to have a nose so big that I couldn't see what was happening at the end of it. That was probably what made Mr Irons give detentions to people who didn't deserve it! Michael saw me and asked what I was doing, so I told him. But he said my nose was too small and flat to ever get in the way of my eyes, so I didn't have anything to worry about.

When we got to Mr Irons' office, Mrs Khan told us to wait outside. We couldn't hear anything except a loud buzzing as if there were two giant bumblebees on the other side of the door. But after a minute, Mr Irons came out and stared down at Michael, the new boy and me with his nose thrust in the air. Maybe he was trying to see if he could see past the end of it better that way.

He gave Josie her football back and didn't say anything else to us, but from that day on, whenever he saw any of us, his eyes would narrow, and his nose would whistle ever so quietly. You don't really need to speak someone else's language to know when they don't like you very much. So even though the new boy couldn't speak many English words then, he knew we had to keep ourselves – and Josie's football – out of the way of Mr Irons, and his horrible whistling nose.

THE UNEXPECTED ADVENTURE

That weekend, I decided I wanted to ask Mum some more of my eleven questions to see if she knew the answers.

I waited until Sunday morning arrived, because that was when I knew Mum wouldn't be too tired and I could ask her lots of things, instead of just one or two things. The only problem is, I had to be extra, extra patient, because every Sunday morning, my mum spends at least one hour reading the Sunday morning paper. It's not a real Sunday paper because Mum never buys them – she says you can buy a whole meal for the price of a Sunday paper these days. So instead, all through the week, she collects two of the biggest newspapers from the reference section of the library, and then on Saturday night, she brings them all home and gets them ready for the next day. She opens them out at the centre and puts them in order – so that Monday's papers are on the top and Saturday's papers are on the bottom, and then folds them together like a big book. It's too heavy to hold up and read twelve big newspapers in one go, so Mum always reads it bent over the kitchen table as if she's doing homework.

I don't like disturbing Mum when she's reading the paper because she only gets to do it once a week, so I quickly finished my toast and milk, and silently stared at her as she finished her breakfast. But grown-ups take an awfully long time eating breakfast when they don't have to go to work, and on this morning, Mum seemed to be moving so slowly that you could hardly call it moving at all. I could hear the ticking of the kitchen clock getting louder and louder and my fingers and legs getting bored of waiting.

As soon as Mum took the last bite of her toast, I decided I couldn't wait for her any longer and asked, 'Mum, where's Syria?'

The question made her look up at me straight away.

71

'What did you say, darling?'

'Just . . . Do you know where Syria is, Mum?' I said, more quietly.

My mum pushed up her glasses and looked at me with her head to one side.

Then she said, 'Syria is a country very far away from here, my love. Why do you want to know?'

I shrugged. 'That's where the new boy in our class is from.'

'Ah,' she said, nodding. 'OK. Tell you what. Why don't you go and get the atlas book and I'll show you?'

I nodded and ran to the living room, trying to remember where I had last put the atlas book. It's hard finding a book in our house because we have so many of them. Mum loves collecting old books and reading them again and again. She takes the copies that are about to be thrown away by her library – so you could say she rescues them. The only problem is, we don't really have space for any more because our rooms are covered with piles of old books. Even the toilet!

The atlas book was big and Mum always kept the very big books on the bottom shelf of our bookcase. So, I climbed over the back of the sofa and crawled down into the narrow gap head first, to see if it was there. Luckily it was! I grabbed it and pulled it out. The atlas book is one of the oldest books in the house and is almost half as tall as me and just as heavy, so I dragged it along behind me into the kitchen and placed it with a bang onto the kitchen table.

I watched as Mum flipped to the index and then to a page near the middle. 'Here you go,' she said, turning the map around to show me. 'This atlas is a little old, but I don't think the borders have changed that much . . .'

I let my finger meet hers where it said the word 'SYRIA' in capital letters, and looked at the strange shape of the country the new boy had run away from. It looked like a woman yawning and wearing a tiara and whose hair was being blown in the wind. Except she was all pointy.

'Mum?'

'Hm?'

'What fruits do people from Syria like the most?' I crossed my fingers and toes hoping that she would know the answer, because if she did, then I would know the answers to three of my original eleven questions! I had found out where the new boy was from and what language he spoke – and as a bonus had seen what his country looked like on a map, *and* learned that he was good at football.

'Well let's see . . . I don't really know . . . I guess the same fruits we do. And exotic ones like dates and pomegranates. Your Aunty Selma used to make chicken with pomegranate seeds, remember?'

I shook my head.

'Ah. Well, it was quite a while ago. It was before your dad . . . had to leave us . . . But I *think* the dish she used to make was a Syrian one. Or was it Lebanese? I can't remember. But here, you see . . .' she said, pointing to a country next to Syria which had the word 'LEBANON' on it. 'Lebanon and Syria are right next door to each other, so I guess they must eat the same kind of fruits.'

'Can we ring and ask her?'

My mum smiled. 'I can ask her the next time she calls. Remember, she lives here now . . .' And Mum pointed to a much larger country lying above Syria called 'TURKEY'. 'It's a bit far and it'll be expensive to call her right now. But listen. We'll go and see her one day soon, and when we do, you can ask her and Uncle Turgay all about it in person!'

I nodded but didn't say anything because I suddenly missed my Aunty Selma an awful lot. It's funny how you can go for long bits of time without even thinking of someone, and then suddenly feel all wrong because you realise they're not around any more. I feel like that about my dad sometimes. It feels horrible when I go to bed and realise that I haven't thought about him all day – not even for a minute. But I always remember him at night before I go to sleep, because that's when he used to tell me stories and do funny patterns on my forehead so that it tickled. It's different with my Aunty Selma though, because she's not my real aunty. So I think it might be OK if I don't think about her every day.

She's my mum's best friend because they like laughing at the same things. She has dimples just like I do, and she always wears lots of sparkling bracelets and necklaces. She used to live two floors below us with Uncle Turgay, and every Sunday night, they would invite Mum and Dad and me down for dinner and give us all sorts of special things to eat – like bread with spinach inside it and a special kind of tea that came in a small glass and didn't have any milk in it. I remember the tea because Dad let me taste it once, but I didn't like it at all!

But then, after Dad died, Aunty Selma and Uncle Turgay said they were leaving because the Economy was being bad. Grown-ups are always talking about the Economy – especially in shops and at bus stops and on the news. And they always sound angry or sad when they talk about it. I hate the Economy because it made Aunty Selma and Uncle Turgay suddenly disappear – just like Dad. They send us pictures and boxes of sweets sometimes in the post. And even though I like getting things from them because the stamps are interesting, I can tell it makes Mum sad. Now there's an old lady living in their flat and she never speaks to anyone. I don't think Mum could be best friends with her even if she wanted to.

I thought about my question again.

'So, people from Syria like pom-e . . . pom-grain . . .'

'Pom-e-gran-ate,' Mum corrected. 'Remember it like . . . let's see . . . One half of a *pom-pom* and a delicious letter "*e*" that your *Gran ate*! Pom-e-gran-ate!'

I nodded and said the word out loud three times. I love it when Mum comes up with ways to help me remember how to spell or say a word. Last year I had to learn the word 'conundrum' for a spelling test but kept forgetting how many nuns or 'n's there were in it. And then Mum told me to close my eyes and picture a man called *Co* and a lonely *nun*, banging on a *drum*. And I've never spelled it wrong since!

I thought about pomegranates and how they might be Ahmet's favourite food and how he might be missing them.

So I asked, 'Mum, can we get one?'

'One what, darling?'

'A pom-e-gran-ate?' I said, carefully.

'Hmmm ... They're a bit expensive ... and you can't find them everywhere ...'

'How expensive?'

'I'm not sure. About one pound fifty I think.'

'What? Nearly two pounds just for one?' I cried out. You could buy a whole packet of colouring pens *and* a rubber for that much money!

Mum laughed. 'Yes, darling. For one. They come a long way to get to our supermarkets. And secondly, a pomegranate is also a really special fruit. It's like millions of tiny fruit all hidden away inside a small ball, and you can eat it for days.'

'Oh . . .' I said, trying hard to think of what millions of one fruit hidden inside a ball would look like.

She looked at me and then smiled. 'Do you want to see if we can find one? Shall we make that our adventure for today?'

I jumped up and nodded. 'But can we get two?' I asked.

'And why would you need two?'

I think Mum already knew the answer because her lips looked like they were about to smile. I didn't think she'd tell me off, even though pomegranates are so expensive, but you can never be too sure with grown-ups. Sometimes they don't tell you off even when you've done something you know you shouldn't have. And at other times, when you think you haven't done anything that bad at all, they punish you twice as much. Michael says it's so they can keep us on our toes. But I've never stood on my toes when I'm being told off so I don't see how that works.

'I want to get two so that I can give one to the new boy,' I said. 'I've been giving him my sherbet lemons and sweets after school, but he didn't like them that much. But then I gave him an apple and an orange, and he liked those better. And Ms Hemsi said that he's from Syria and that he only speaks . . . he only speaks . . .' I hesitated, trying to remember what Ms Hemsi had said.

'Arabic?' Mum asked, trying to help.

I shook my head. 'Cur . . . Cur . . . Curt-wish . . .' I guessed, knowing it was wrong.

'Ah. Kurdish . . .'

I nodded.

'I see . . .' I could tell Mum was interested in what I was saying because she had leaned back in her chair and folded her arms

'And I thought maybe he'd like a fruit he used to have at home all the time – before the bullies dropped bombs on everything and made him run away.'

I stopped, worried that Mum would think that it was silly and maybe a waste of money buying food only to give it away. But she didn't. Instead she said, 'I think that's a brilliant idea! Go and get ready, and we'll head out on a pomegranate hunt!'

I got ready so quickly that morning that I think I must have beaten a world record. In five minutes I had pulled on my adventure jeans and my old Tintin jumper, packed my rucksack with a water bottle, an apple and a banana, put on my wellies, brushed my hair AND emptied my piggy bank. I had exactly four pounds and twenty pence saved up, so I took three pounds, hoping that, just like my astronaut stationery set, I could find two pomegranates that were on sale.

First, we went to the fruit stall that was at the bottom of our high street. It's run by a man and a woman called Mr and Mrs Marbles who like to shout 'Only a paaaaan! Fruit and veg, only a paaaaaan' to all the people that walk by. Their faces are always red and smiling, and they wear giant square-shaped green belts around their waist, which look empty but jingle loudly when they walk.

Mrs Marbles helps people pick out the fruit they want, and Mr Marbles puts them in a bag. We always buy our fruit and vegetables from them and I've never known them not to have anything we need. But when we asked them if they had a pomegranate, they both shook their heads at us and told us to try the supermarket.

So, we walked up and over the hill to the

supermarket. They had a fruit section that was as long as our house, but Mum couldn't see a pomegranate anywhere. We went over to a man who was stacking carrots and humming to himself and asked him if they had any pomegranates in store. He walked us over to a small box, but it was empty.

'Sorry, love, looks like we've run out. You might want to try the bigger supermarket on the other side of town.'

'Ah. OK. Thank you.' Mum looked down at me and sighed. Then she said, 'Come on! The adventure continues!'

We hopped onto a bus and after half an hour, landed at an even *bigger* supermarket. This one had a car park as big as a football field and corridors as long as the ones in school! But we still couldn't find a pomegranate anywhere.

'Let's ask someone!' said Mum. 'They must have them . . .'

We walked around and found a man dressed in a suit who was standing by the sandwich section. He had a label on his jacket that said, 'Frank Smith, Floor Manager'. I didn't know what a Floor Manager was, but I guessed he had to make sure the floor was clean and help anyone who fell down get back up again. But Mr Smith didn't look like the kind of person who would help anyone get up from a floor. He had lips that went downwards as if they'd never smiled, and his hair looked wet as if a large bottle of oil had fallen on top of it. He was staring at a clipboard and muttering angrily to himself.

'Excuse me . . . Frank, is it? Hi,' said Mum, smiling.

The man gave my mum a cold nod before continuing to fill in a long form.

'We're looking for some pomegranates but can't seem to find any,' said Mum, smiling even more.

'We don't sell them here,' said Frank, still looking at his clipboard.

'Oh really? Any idea where we could find some?' continued Mum.

'No.'

My mum looked at him for a few seconds and then said, in her warmest voice, 'Thank you. You've really outdone yourself in helping us today. Have a wonderful day!' And grabbing my hand, she walked away.

'Mum, why were you so nice to him?' I asked. 'He

was horrible! He didn't try and help us even a little bit!'

'Because you should never be horrible to someone who's being horrible to you,' said Mum. 'Otherwise they win by making you just as bad as them. Now, come on. Let's get back on the bus! There's another place I know we can try.'

By this time, I was getting hungry, so while we were waiting for the next bus, I ate my banana.

'Hmmm . . .' said my mum, looking at her watch. It was nearly two o'clock and there were some dark grey clouds gathering in the sky. 'I'm afraid the next stop will have to be our last one, darling. It looks like it's going to start raining in a bit.'

A few seconds later, a very full bus pulled up in front of us and we squeezed on. I clung to Mum's coat because there weren't any empty seats and waited for our stop. I was worried, because if this was our last try, then I had just one chance left to find a pomegranate – so I crossed my fingers and my toes, and made a wish that we would.

The next place felt like an awfully long way away, and when we finally got there, it was filled with so many people that we could hardly walk properly. There were lots and lots of market stalls lying in the middle of a big road, all selling fish and meat and bedsheets and long gold chains. There was a man with a microphone who was trying to sell perfumes like a gameshow host by shouting, 'Roll up! Roll up!' And next to him was a woman shouting, 'Peter never picked potatoes as good as these before! Buy 'em now before they go!' I wondered who Peter was and how much money he made picking potatoes, but then I could smell onions and burgers being cooked somewhere which made my tummy rumble. I love burgers – especially ones that have lots of fried onions and ketchup in them. But I wanted to save my money for the pomegranates, so I scrunched up my nose and tried not to smell anything at all.

We visited every stall in the market, from the beginning of the street right to the end, but even though we looked as carefully as we could, we couldn't find a single pomegranate anywhere. My mum had told me to look for a pinkish ball that looked like a very hard apple and which had a small crown on the top. But I couldn't see anything that looked even a little bit royal.

'Try the store up by the station,' suggested one of the stall owners when Mum asked her for help. 'They have everything under the sun in there. They should have some.'

'Thank you,' said Mum. She grabbed my hand and gave it a squeeze because she could tell I was starting to give up hope. 'Nearly there,' she whispered. 'I can feel it.'

We walked for five minutes down the road and up to the station and found the shop the woman in the market had told us about. It was much smaller than the big supermarket with Frank the horrible Floor Manager in it, but it was bright with lots of coloured lights and bowls and bowls of fruit and vegetables outside. It had everything you could think of – peaches and plums, mangoes and bananas, kiwis and pears, yellow apples and red apples and pink apples and even a spiky pink and green fruit that I had never seen before. But we couldn't see any pomegranates, so we went inside and Mum asked the man standing behind the counter.

'Ah!' nodded the man, scratching the tip of his nose. 'Pomegranate! I see for you . . .' And talking out loud to himself, he hurried to a corner of the shop and quickly looked through some boxes.

'Much, much regret!' he called out, holding up an empty box. 'No more. But we have delivery on Tuesday!'

The man came back and looked at us and we looked at him. He had a large white beard, a moustache that was curly at the ends, and was wearing a bright red turban. I liked him because his eyebrows were like hairy caterpillars and they jumped up and down a lot when he spoke.

'Oh well,' said Mum. 'We tried, at least.'

The man looked at me. I think he must have noticed that I was looking sad, because he said, 'It is for little one?'

I looked up and nodded. 'And for my friend,' I said. 'He's new in my class and misses home and that's what he used to have.'

'I see,' he said, looking at me with a smile. Then he frowned as if he had just thought of something, and suddenly pointing his finger at the ceiling and crying out, 'A-HA!', he ran to a small door at the back of the shop and disappeared.

Mum and I looked at each other in surprise.

'He's funny,' I said. 'I like him.'

'He seems lovely,' agreed Mum.

After a few seconds, the man came back, but instead of returning to the counter, he came and stood in front of us.

'They are not perfect, but will be OK,' he said. And whipping his hands out from behind his back, he held up two little pink balls that each had a crown on top.

'Oh!' cried out Mum, clapping her hands. 'You have some!'

'They are little old – my wife, she says they are not perfect one hundred per cent, so we don't sell you see?' said the man, his eyebrows jumping up and down even more. 'My wife – she knows everything about fruit, so I listen to her most!'

'They're perfect enough for us!' laughed Mum. 'Aren't they, darling?'

I nodded as the man gently handed them to me.

'You and friend enjoy please,' he whispered, and tapped me on the nose with a finger that had a golden ring with a large red stone on it.

I looked down at the pomegranates. They were the size of grapefruits and had a hard peachy-pink and brown skin that was as smooth and as shiny as polished glass. And both of them had a tiny flower on the top made up of exactly seven stiff brown petals. They were the best, most interesting things I had ever seen.

Mum took out her purse because that's where I had put my pocket money, but the man shook his head and waved his hand.

'No, no. You must not! It is gift for little one!'

'Oh! No – you *must* let me—'

But the man held up his hands which made Mum go quiet and then put a hand on his chest. 'It is gift. They are not excellent. Not new. So very poor gift.'

'They're the BEST gifts,' said Mum. 'Aren't they, darling?'

I nodded, feeling so happy that I wanted to hug the man and Mum and jump up and down all at once.

'Thank you, Sir,' I said, giving the man an enormous smile.

'Welcome, welcome,' he said. And, smiling back, he gave me a pat on the top of my head and waved at us as we left the shop.

'What a wonderful man,' said Mum, as she helped me put the pomegranates in my rucksack.

'He looked like a king,' I said, thinking of the ring with the stone in it and his red turban.

Mum laughed. 'He certainly has the heart of one! Maybe he is one! You never can tell with people! Now. Seeing as our Unexpected Adventure is at an end, let's hurry home before it starts to pour!'

I looked up. Everything had suddenly turned dark and the sky was filled with large grey clouds that were so low you could hear them rumbling. But I didn't care, because I had two of the best presents I could ever have in my bag, given to me by a man with the heart of a king.

THE BIG FIGHT

The next morning, I told Josie, Michael and Tom about the Unexpected Adventure my mum had taken me on, and they all said they wanted to come with me next time and meet the man in the red turban with the king's heart too. None of them had ever seen the inside of a pomegranate before, so I tried to describe the colour and shapes of the seeds to them on the bus to school. But they still looked confused, so I drew them this picture on the back of my exercise book instead:

I think pomegranates are now my most favourite fruit in the whole wide world. Not just because of the way they taste, but because of how they look. On the outside they look like extra-shiny balls that have been dipped into a bucket of sunset colours, like peach and pink and gold. But the inside is even cooler, because when you pull one open, it's like finding a million sparkling red rubies all squashed together inside a round suitcase and bursting to get out.

'You have to push each one out gently,' Mum had said, when she had cut mine open and shown me how to pop the seeds out. 'See? As if you're plucking out jewels from the roof of a cave!' She showed me how to peel off the skin lying between the seeds too – but I didn't like that part so much because the peelings looked like bits of old snake-skin that I'd seen in a zoo once.

I meant to give the pomegranate to the new boy at home-time, but I was so excited that I couldn't wait until then. So as soon as the bell for first break began to ring, I hid the pomegranate under my school jumper and hurried out into the playground with it. We're not allowed to take food into the playground because we're only supposed to eat snacks in the dinner hall. But I wasn't going to eat it or make anyone else eat it, so I didn't think it counted.

The new boy followed us out because he knew we were his friends now. He had stopped disappearing every break-time and only went to have his Seclusion during lunch-times. Even Ms Hemsi had stopped coming out during first breaks and went to the staff room, which I think meant she knew we were the new boy's friends too.

'Here!' I said as soon we got into our corner of the playground. And pulling the pomegranate out from under my jumper, I held it out to him. 'It's for you!'

Josie and Michael looked at each other and Tom

looked at me, as we all waited for the new boy to say something. But he just stared and stared – first at us and then the pomegranate – and didn't say or do anything.

'Knew you should have put a sticker on it!' whispered Tom, shaking his head.

Then, slowly, the new boy reached out and took the pomegranate in his hands.

'Home,' he said quietly, his lion eyes getting very big. 'I . . . have . . . home . . .'

'Yes!' I said. 'Your home in Syria! I've seen it. On a map. You know, MAP?'

The new boy fell quiet. And then, for the first time since we had met him, he smiled. Not a small smile, or a side-smile or even a half-smile, but a real, proper smile that went from one cheek to the other, and which made his eyes smile too. He opened his mouth to say something when, suddenly, Brendan-the-Bully pushed past us.

'Gimme that!' he said, and he snatched the pomegranate from Ahmet's hands.

'Give that BACK!' I shouted, feeling scared and angry all at once.

'Make me!' sneered Brendan-the-Bully as he turned around to face me.

I don't know why, but sometimes, when someone you don't like looks at you right in the eyes, they suddenly seem to grow taller and you suddenly seem to grow shorter – even when, really, you're both the same size. Usually it's only for a few seconds and then you grow back to your normal height again. But sometimes it goes on for so long that you wonder if you'll ever get back to the height you used to be.

This was one of those times. When Brendan-the-Bully turned to look at me, he stared into my eyes so hard and for so long that he seemed to grow by at least two more inches. But I was feeling so hot and angry that I could feel my ears going red and I didn't care. I took a step forward and tried to grab the pomegranate back.

'Go on! Try again!' laughed Brendan-the-Bully, as he whipped it away and held it high above his head. I could feel my face getting redder and redder and my legs getting shorter and shorter as I tried to jump and snatch it back from him. Then suddenly, he threw the pomegranate to Chris, who was standing behind me. Chris caught it and tossed it up and down in one hand, waiting for one of us to try and do something. Josie and

Tom and Michael all lunged forward but Chris was too quick, and threw the pomegranate to Liam, who quickly threw it back to Brendan-the-Bully.

This might have carried on all break-time, because Brendan-the-Bully likes playing this game and no one has ever beaten him at it. But then what happened next was so unexpected, so shocking and so fantastic that even Brendan-the-Bully didn't know what to do!

Because suddenly, with a huge roar, Ahmet ran straight at Brendan-the-Bully, and like an angry lion, crashed into him with his head! Brendan-the-Bully fell backwards and onto the floor, his legs swinging up into the air. We all gasped out loud, but Ahmet didn't stop there.

He jumped on top, with his face red and patchy, and punched Brendan-the-Bully as many times as he could, shouting something that none of us could understand. Someone behind us cried out 'FIIIIIGHT!' and everyone in the playground ran over to watch. But – and this was the most shocking thing of all! – it wasn't really a fight. You need two people – at least – to be fighting for it to be a fight. And Brendan-the-Bully WASN'T FIGHTING BACK! Not at all! Not even for a second! Instead he was holding his arms over his face as Ahmet continued punching and roaring and shouting at him with all his might.

'BREAK IT UP NOW!' shouted a voice as the crowd parted, and Mr Irons and Mrs Sanders came running through.

But Ahmet wouldn't stop. He was like a machine that didn't have an off-button and he continued to punch and punch and punch just as hard and as fast as he could.

'RIGHT, YOUNG MAN!' cried Mr Irons. And, grabbing him by the back of his jumper, Mr Irons lifted Ahmet up off Brendan-the-Bully, whilst Mrs Sanders pulled Brendan-the-Bully back onto his feet.

Everyone fell quiet, but I don't know if that was because we were all wondering what was going to happen next, or because none of us could believe that Brendan-the-Bully had actually been hurt. His face was bright red and his eyes looked watery, and there were tiny stones from the playground floor stuck to the sides of his cheeks.

With a horrible glint in his eye, Mr Irons stared down at Ahmet and shouted, 'WHAT DO YOU THINK YOU'RE DOING, BOY? EH? EH?'

Ahmet stared angrily at the floor and didn't say anything.

'WHO STARTED THIS?' shouted out Mrs Sanders, who was so angry that she had forgotten to look over her glasses and was looking at everyone straight through them instead.

I immediately pointed to Brendan-the-Bully, and so did Tom and Josie and Michael.

'RIGHT! ALL OF YOU! WITH ME! NOW!' ordered Mrs Sanders, dragging Brendan-the-Bully by the arm across the playground and into the school.

Mr Irons flicked his hand and pointed to the doors, his nose whistling louder than it had ever whistled before. I followed Tom and Josie and Michael as we all hung our heads and made our way through the crowds. Everyone stared at us, and then stared at Ahmet. His face was even redder than mine and his lion eyes were so big and wet it looked as if they were drowning. He wiped away an angry tear and looked back over his shoulder. I looked back too and saw lots of bright pink spots all over the ground.

The pomegranate had smashed open, and all its ruby red seeds had been crushed beneath everyone's feet.

97

After we told Mrs Sanders all about what had happened, she gave me fifty lines to do for taking the pomegranate out into the playground, and said that Ahmet and Brendan-the-Bully had to write lines every night for the rest of the week with Mr Irons. We tried to tell her and Mrs Khan that the fight wasn't Ahmet's fault and that sometimes, hitting someone when they're being horrible and taking something that's yours away from you, can make you feel a hundred times better than just telling a teacher ever would. Even a million times better! But they just shook their heads and said that Ahmet should never have hit Brendan-the-Bully. We didn't say anything after that because sometimes you can tell when grown-ups won't listen to you any more. Usually they say, 'That's an end of it' or 'I've said my peas' or 'That's that'. But teachers always say, 'That's all. You can leave now.'

As we left, I told Ahmet that I was sorry for getting him into trouble and that I would try and find another pomegranate for him. All he did was give me a nod and a thumbs-up. I think it was his way of telling me not to worry and that being able to roar like a lion on top of a bully was worth doing lines for. Even if it was hundreds of them, in a language he didn't know how to speak yet.

As we all went home that afternoon, we talked about the Big Fight, and how Ahmet was going to be famous because he was the first boy ever to have beaten up Brendan-the-Bully.

'You wait and see,' said Tom. 'Everyone's going to want to be his friend now! Even the cool kids!'

I guessed Tom was right, but it made me feel sad. If Ahmet made friends with the cool kids, that meant he wouldn't talk to us or play football with us any more. There's a law that says cool kids can only ever hang out with other cool kids, and that they mustn't ever talk to us – except for when they're put in a group with us by a teacher. I don't know who wrote the law, but Michael knows all about it. I guess his mum must have told him.

But it turned out Michael was wrong about the law. Because Ahmet never stopped being our friend. Not even after he became the most popular boy in school for beating up Brendan-the-Bully.

And not even when all the newspapers in the world made him the Most Famous Refugee Boy on the planet.

10

WAR AND MISSING PIECES

On the day after the Big Fight, just as Tom had guessed, Ahmet became famous. In the playground, wherever he went, people pointed and gasped and called him 'The Boy Who Beat Brendan-the-Bully', and they asked him lots of questions like, 'Is it true you can do a hundred punches in under a minute?' and 'What were you REALLY fighting over – was it your parents' ransom money?' and 'When are you gonna fight again? Can we come and watch?'

After a while, Ms Hemsi began to tell everyone to leave Ahmet alone, so everyone started asking Michael and Josie and Tom and me their questions instead. I didn't say much and neither did Michael. But Josie and Tom got so excited that they started to add new bits to the story, so that by the end of the week, most of the school believed Ahmet hadn't just beaten up Brendan-the-Bully, but had fought Chris and Liam too, over a suitcase full of red diamonds – and a pink basketball.

All of this made Brendan-the-Bully scowl more than ever. But even though he stared at us all the time and Chris and Liam showed us their fists whenever they saw us, they didn't chase us around the playground, or steal Josie's football, or smash into us when we were carrying our lunch trays like we thought they would.

'I bet he's scared of us now that we've got Ahmet,' grinned Tom.

'Yeah!' said Josie. 'He's a proper scaredy-cat now!'

But Michael said he didn't like it one little bit, and that he bet Brendan-the-Bully was up to something. At first, I didn't believe him, but then lots of strange things began to happen to Ahmet.

The first thing happened just two days after the Big Fight. We had all been decorating a new pot for our photosynthesis plants, and Mrs Khan had given Ahmet a golden star because his plant had grown faster than anyone else's. I think that was because every morning, before Mrs Khan called the register, he would water it and talk to it for one whole minute. I didn't know that plants could speak different languages, but when I asked Mrs Khan about it, she said plants could speak every language under the sun, and that the more languages they heard, the faster they grew.

Ahmet was really proud of his golden star, and he got a silver one too for decorating his pot with pictures of sea shells and whales and fish. But when we got back from last break that afternoon, his pot was lying broken on the floor and his plant had been stamped on. Someone must have smashed it on purpose because nobody else's plant pots were hurt at all. Mrs Khan said that if the person who did it didn't put their hand up right away, they would be in Big Trouble. But nobody did put their hands up, so The Mystery of the Murdered Plant Pot stayed a mystery.

Then, almost exactly a week after The Mystery of the Murdered Plant Pot, came The Day of the Deathly Worm Tray. After assembly one morning, Mrs Khan told us all to get our workbooks from our class trays. But when Ahmet pulled his open, he found it bursting with a whole pile of large, fat, wriggling worms! He cried out and dropped the tray on the floor so that all the worms went flying out across the room. That made Dean – who sits on the table behind me – be sick all over his table. Dean is scared of anything that doesn't have any legs on it – even snails. But he hates worms the worst.

Mr Whittaker, the school cleaner, had to come and clean it all up, and Mrs Khan and Ms Hemsi were very angry and checked all our trays. But no one else had a single worm in their tray – not even Tony-the-Nose-Picker, who likes to collect all kinds of strange things in his tray. Mrs Khan told the person who had done it to put their hand up again – and this time she looked at Brendan-the-Bully as if she wasn't really speaking to any of us and only to him. But again, nobody put their hand up. So, Mrs Khan shook her head and said she was going to make sure that whoever it was would be caught soon and punished not just by her, but Mrs Sanders too.

And then, after that, came the worst trick of all – the one that everyone in school later called The Great Baked Beans Bag Trap.

Every morning, right before Mrs Khan takes the register, everyone has to put their school bag on their own special hook at the back of the class, and we're only allowed to take our P.E. kit or homework or lunch boxes out when we're told to. Everyone knows whose bag is where, because everyone's hook has their name on top. Just days after The Day of the Deathly Worm Tray, Mrs Khan told us to get up and collect our P.E. kits from our bags, just like she always did on Wednesdays. But when Ahmet went to get his P.E. kit and unzipped his rucksack, a lumpy river of baked beans burst out and splodged and splashed all over him! Everyone cried out 'Eeeeeewwwwwww!' and then instantly fell silent. Mrs Khan was so angry when no one put their hand up again that she cancelled P.E. and Mrs Sanders came and told the whole class off. It was horrible – especially because Ahmet started to cry when he saw what had happened to his P.E. kit and his bag.

I think everyone knew it was Brendan-the-Bully who had done all these things, but no one could prove it. Not even Mrs Khan. After that day, the door to the classroom was locked every break-time and at lunch-time, which stopped anything else from happening to Ahmet's things. But I wanted more than anything for

Brendan-the-Bully to be caught and to prove he was a Criminal, so Michael brought his grandad's magnifying glass in and we all searched for clues. But we couldn't find a single one! Not even in the school bins.

Ahmet was more upset about The Great Baked Beans Bag Trap than any of the other things that had happened. And even though Ms Hemsi washed his rucksack with lots of washing-up liquid, it looked even worse than before and smelled strange too. But Ahmet still brought it into school every day. I wanted to know why he didn't get a new one, or why Ms Hemsi kept saying that it looked fine when it didn't. And then, just two days after The Great Baked Beans Bag Trap, I found out.

We had all put away our books and were getting ready for group story time just like we always did on Fridays, when Mrs Khan made a surprise announcement.

'Now, everyone!' she said. 'This is our last afternoon before we all break up for the half-term holidays, and I thought we could do with a treat! Instead of us all reading a story together, we're going to listen to one instead. And it's a very important story, because it's going to be told to us by someone very special in our class.' Looking over at Ahmet and Ms Hemsi, she waved them over to where she was standing. I didn't know it just then, but I was about to have nearly ALL of my original eleven questions answered in one go!

We all turned around to watch as Ms Hemsi picked up a large pile of papers from the table and followed Ahmet to the front of the class.

'I want everyone to listen extra carefully, and I don't want anyone asking any questions until after Ahmet has finished telling his story. Is that understood?'

'Yes, Mrs Khaaaaaan,' shouted the class.

'Good!' And leaning against her desk, Mrs Khan smiled and said, 'Ahmet . . .?'

Everyone shuffled in their chairs and sat up straight, waiting for Ahmet to speak. I wondered if he would tell the story in English or in Kurdish, but I was so excited I didn't really care.

'Hello. My name is Ahmet. I am nine . . . years old. And I am refugee. I come from Syria.'

As he said this, he pointed to Ms Hemsi, who held up a drawing showing a house and a tree and a car in front of some mountains. And in the front of the car were four people, labelled, 'Me', 'Mum', 'Dad' and 'Sister' – and a cat.

This was the drawing:

I was surprised because I had never thought about Ahmet having a brother or a sister. I thought he was like me and didn't have any. His sister wasn't at our school. In the picture, she looked smaller than him, so maybe she was in nursery.

'But in Syria, there is big war,' said Ahmet, and he pointed to Ms Hemsi again, who held up another picture. This one showed buildings on fire and bombs dropping from a plane and lots of people lying on the ground and other people holding guns.

It looked like this:

Josie stopped chewing her hair and looked at me and then looked back at the drawing again. And from behind, I heard someone whisper, 'Woah! He's seen a real bomb AND a real gun!'

'Because of war, my family ... run away,' said Ahmet, as his lion eyes became big and round and watery. 'We went ... on mountain and rivers ... and carry bags and cat.'

This time, Ms Hemsi held up a picture showing a family crossing mountains and rivers, and in the sky, birds that were crying. In the picture, Ahmet had drawn himself carrying a red rucksack with a black stripe on it, just like the one he had now. That was when I knew why he loved it so much, and why he cried when it had been filled with Brendan-the-Bully's horrible baked beans. He had carried it all the way from his house and over a mountain, which meant it was lots more important and lots more special than any of our bags.

This was the picture:

'Then nowhere safe, so we get on boat on big sea.'

This time, Ms Hemsi held up a drawing of a boat. But the boat wasn't like a normal boat with sails and pointy ends and wooden sides. This one was flat and round and was orange on the sides – just like the ones I had seen on the news that didn't have any toilets on them. And inside the boat were lots of people, all wearing vests that made them look like puffin birds. But there were people in the water too, and they had bubbles coming out of their mouths saying, 'HELP ME'.

Everyone leaned forward in their chairs and tried to read the labels Ahmet had put over some of the people's heads. I saw 'Me' and 'Mum' and 'Dad', but there wasn't one for 'Sister' or 'Cat'. I know cats don't like water because Josie has a cat and she says it screams whenever it rains and always wants to stay inside. So maybe Ahmet's cat didn't want to get into the boat. And maybe his sister didn't want to leave it behind, so she stayed behind to look after it.

This was the boat picture:

'Then we are in another country, called Greece,' said Ahmet. 'We live in tent with lots of people who run away like me. They come from lots of country like Afghanistan and Pakistan and Eritrea.'

The next picture showed a flag with blue and white stripes and a white cross in a blue corner, and next to it were lots of tents and people everywhere sitting next to fires and sleeping on the floor. In this picture, only the words 'Me' and 'Dad' could be seen. Ahmet's mum must be sleeping inside one of the tents.

This was the picture:

'Then we walk long time . . . In lots of country. It was cold, and we sleep on floor. And then we stay in France.'

This time, Ahmet pointed to the next picture with his finger and showed us the railway tracks he had drawn. On it were people carrying suitcases and children, and all of them were walking to a wall with barbed wire on the top. Everyone looked sad. And in the corner, there were army tanks and soldiers holding guns, and all the guns were pointing at the people with the suitcases and children.

Ms Hemsi held this drawing up for longer than any of the others, because Ahmet was looking at it and didn't seem to want to stop staring at it.

This was the drawing:

'Then I come here . . . and come to school. I like here . . . no bombs. It safe and I like new friends and teacher and play football.'

Ahmet stood and stared at everyone, and everyone stared back. Mrs Khan blew her nose loudly, and Ms Hemsi put the drawings down and gave Ahmet a hug.

'Thank you, Ahmet,' said Mrs Khan, standing up and putting a hand on his shoulder. 'Everyone, let's give Ahmet a huge round of applause for being so brave and for sharing his story with us.'

We all clapped, but we didn't clap as loud as we usually do for stories, because I think we were feeling strange. I don't think any of us had ever heard a story like it before. And as sad and as scary as it was, it was even sadder and scarier because it wasn't just a made-up story from one of our reading books. It was all real. Ahmet had survived everything his pictures had shown us and was here. With us. Knowing that made me feel sorry and proud and scared for him all at once; but most of all, it made me want to tell him he was definitely the bravest person I knew.

'Now, as you have seen, Ahmet's story is very special, and I'm sure you have lots of questions you want to ask him,' said Mrs Khan. Everyone's hands immediately shot up into the air – but I think mine was first.

'That's wonderful!' smiled Mrs Khan, as she signalled at us to put our hands back down. 'But as Ahmet is still learning his English words, we're only going to ask him three questions. I want you all to write down just one question for him on a piece of paper.' Mrs Khan walked around and gave us each a thin slip of blank paper. 'And when you're done, Ms Hemsi is going to pick out three questions we can ask him. You have a few minutes to think of your question and to write it out in your very best handwriting. Try to get all your spellings right, and remember, just *one* question each.'

The entire class fell quiet as everyone grabbed their pencils, put their heads down and wrote out their questions. I had lots of questions that I wanted to ask, but I picked the one that was most new and wrote that one out. After a few minutes, Mrs Khan said our time was up, and Ms Hemsi collected all the bits of paper.

Everyone began to whisper to one another as Mrs Khan and Ms Hemsi looked through our questions and either shook their heads or nodded.

'What did you ask?' whispered Tom, turning around.

'I asked why he didn't stay in Greece, because the weather's warmer there and they have more seaside places,' whispered back Josie.

'Oh. I asked how fast he had to run to get away from the bombs,' whispered Tom.

'Michael, what did you ask?' whispered Josie, leaning forward and poking Michael on the shoulder.

'I asked if it was scary to be in the boat and if he was on it at night-time,' said Michael.

'That's two questions!' whispered Josie, shaking her head. Then she looked at me. 'What did you ask?'

'I asked what happened to his cat and what his sister's name is,' I answered.

'Oh!' said Tom. 'But that's two questions as well!'

'Right, everyone!' said Mrs Khan, clapping her hands so that we all stopped whispering and looked to the front of the class. 'We have some excellent questions here, but we've chosen three. I'm going to say them in English, and then Ms Hemsi is going to translate both the question and answer for us. Right ... the first question is: what did your mum and dad do in Syria?'

Ms Hemsi spoke to Ahmet in Kurdish and he said something back. Ms Hemsi nodded and then looking at us, said, 'Ahmet's father was a teacher. And his mother wrote for a newspaper.'

Everyone in class nodded and we waited for Mrs Khan to read out the next question. I crossed my fingers extra-tight in the hopes that it would be mine.

'The next question is: what did you like doing most before the war happened?'

We waited for Ms Hemsi to tell Ahmet what the question was and then reply. 'He liked to play football with his friends,' answered Ms Hemsi. 'And going to the park with his grandfather and eating kibbeh.' She smiled at Ahmet, and before any of us could ask what a 'kibbeh' was, explained, 'A kibbeh is a very special snack which is filled with minced meat in the middle and is covered with lots of delicious spices. It's very famous in Syria and it looks like . . .'

Ms Hemsi went over to the blackboard and quickly drew a shape. It looked like a small American football.

'Is that the right shape, Ahmet?' she asked.

Ahmet nodded. We all looked at each other and tried to imagine what an American football with minced meat in the middle might taste like.

As Mrs Khan held up the last slip of paper, I decided

to cross both my toes and fingers. But it didn't work, because then she said, 'And the last question is: do you still sleep in a tent or do you sleep in a house now?'

When Ahmet heard this question from Ms Hemsi, he shook his head and said something.

'No, he sleeps in a house now,' said Ms Hemsi. 'And he is happy because there is a toilet in it and hot water and food.'

As we all nodded to each other, Mrs Khan put her arm around Ahmet and said, 'Let's give Ahmet another round of applause, shall we?'

This time, nearly everyone clapped much louder than before and Michael even cried out, 'Woooooohooooo!' as Ahmet and Ms Hemsi went and sat back down. But I could see Brendan-the-Bully mouthing 'Booooo!' and making a face as if something smelled, and Liam giving a double thumbs-down. I looked back at Mrs Khan and Ms Hemsi hoping they had seen too, but they were busy looking at Ahmet.

'Right! Now everyone, before we leave today, I want you all to listen to me very carefully.' Mrs Khan clapped her hands once and waited for everyone to settle back down. 'As I said, you all had some fantastic questions for

Ahmet, and I'm very proud of you for thinking up such interesting and thoughtful ones too. But . . .' And here she looked at us with her eyebrows raised, which meant she was being extra-serious and would be extra-angry if we didn't listen to her. 'I'm sure I don't have to tell you that running away from a war and leaving your home is a very hard thing to do. And it's especially hard when you have to try and put all the missing pieces of your life back together again, in a place that's new and strange to you.'

Then Mrs Khan quickly glanced at me and Josie and Michael and Tom and said, 'I know that some of you miss Ahmet when he's not allowed to go out and play. And I know you all have lots of questions for him. But it's very important that he talks to people who know what he's been through, and who can help him feel better. And it's even *more* important that they can ask him the kinds of questions you all want to ask him, in a safe and secluded space *first,* before he's ready to speak to other people more. OK?'

Josie looked over at me and I looked over at her and Tom and Michael looked over their shoulders at us. So *that* was what the Seclusion was for! It was so that Ahmet could talk to people!

'So,' continued Mrs Khan. 'I want you all to promise me that you won't ask Ahmet any more questions about the war – or about his family – without asking me or Ms Hemsi first. Is that understood?'

'Yes, Mrs Khaaaaaan . . .' said the class, as the bell for home-time began to ring.

'Good! Now, row one, put away your things and off you go. Make sure you all have everything you need for your homework assignments for the half-term, and I'll see you in a week's time!'

As we waited for our row to be called out, I looked over my shoulder at Ahmet and wondered what pieces he was still missing before he could put his life back together again. It was like a jigsaw, I thought. I hate doing jigsaws – even the easy ones, because I always get bored halfway through, and I couldn't imagine trying to do one that had pieces missing.

I sure hoped that when he was running away from all the bullies and the bombs, Ahmet hadn't lost any of the important pieces on the way. And that, if he had, someone was helping him find new ones that were exactly the right shape and colours that he needed.

THE GAME OF SCRABBLE

After hearing Ahmet's story and seeing his pictures, I was bursting with lots of new questions. So were Tom and Josie and Michael, but we knew we couldn't ask Ahmet anything.

'We should write them down,' suggested Josie. 'Then maybe after the holidays Ahmet will have put some more pieces back together, and Mrs Khan will think it's OK for us to ask him?'

We all agreed, so when I got home that night, I took out my old list of questions and, after crossing out the ones I had the answers to, wrote the new questions out in my very best handwriting – just to make sure we wouldn't forget any of them.

This is what the list looked like:

My 11 Questions

1. Where did you have to run away from?
2. What language do you speak?
3. Who's the woman in the red scarf?
4. Do you have any brothers or sisters?
5. What did the bullies do to make you run away?
6. Did you have to get on a boat like the people on the news?
7. What sports do you like best?
8. What's your favourite fruit?
9. How far did you have to walk to get away from the bullies?
10. Do you like it here or do you miss your old house more?
11. Do you have a best friend?

Our 5 New Questions

1. What is your sister's name (and where is she now)?
2. Why wasn't your mum in the last picture?
3. What happened to the cat?
4. How long did it take to walk to France?
5. Who are the bullies who dropped bombs on your house?

121

After I had finished writing them out, I put the list in the front pocket of my rucksack. I would have to wait until the holiday was over to find out if Ahmet was ready to answer any of them.

I know everyone in school likes the holidays, but I don't. Not really. Mum still has to work and she can't afford to send me to a holiday camp or for extra activities, so I have to spend most of my time with Mrs Abbey. Usually Michael and Josie's parents come and take me to their house for a day, but Michael's parents were taking him on a holiday to France, and Josie was going camping, and Tom and his brothers were visiting family near the seaside, so there was no one to play with this holiday. The week felt extra long and extra boring, because London had what Mum calls a 'Grey Day Week'. That's when all the days are so cold and grey and wet and blustery that you don't want to get out of your pyjamas or your bed, and the whole week feels like one long grey day that you can't wait to be over.

But on the Sunday morning before school opened again, just as Mum was reading her newspapers and I was trying to decide what we should do for our Sunday Adventure, the phone rang. Mum picked it up and when she put it back down again, she was biting her lip and frowning. That meant she had forgotten something important and was feeling angry at herself.

'Darling, I'm so sorry – I completely forgot! But that was your Uncle Lenny on the phone reminding me that he's coming to lunch today.'

I jumped up in excitement.

'With your Aunt Christina and Baby Jacob . . .' she added.

I sat back down and made a face. 'Can't Uncle Lenny just come on his own?' I asked.

Mum shook her head. 'No, he can't. Your aunt and Jacob haven't been here in a while, so it's nice that they want to come.' And then noticing that I was still making a face, she added, 'And guess what? Uncle Lenny is bringing lunch – roast chicken! Your favourite! AND he said he wants a Scrabble match so you're to set the board up *immediately*!'

I jumped up and ran to my bedroom to get the Scrabble board from underneath my bed. I love Scrabble more than all the other board games, because it's the only game that I don't ever get bored playing. Dad always used to let me win by placing his letters in silly places so that he would get the lowest points. But Mum and Uncle Lenny never play low-scoring words on purpose, because Mum says that helping me to win is cheating. She does let me use the dictionary though – because otherwise it wouldn't be fair. After all, she and Uncle Lenny are older and cleverer and know lots more words than a nine-and-three-quarters-year-old could ever know.

And just like that, I didn't mind Aunt Christina and Jacob coming at all! Because there was nothing I loved better than eating my Uncle Lenny's roast chicken. Except playing Scrabble with him.

Just like Josie, Uncle Lenny is in all my memories too. When Dad died, I remember him being at the hospital with us and hugging Mum and me a lot. That was when he started calling me his 'brave little tiger'. I don't know why, because I didn't feel even the tiniest bit brave.

But I didn't mind. Because after the Funeral, he was the only person who stayed behind and helped Mum sort everything out. None of my other uncles and aunts who visited us that day ever came back to see Mum and me again. Mum's friends try and visit us when they can, and Josie's mum is always asking us if we need any help, but they're busy with work just like Mum is.

Sometimes I think most of the people who came to the Funeral were all really witches and wizards who had appeared out of thin air, just so they could eat a buffet and shake their heads a lot before disappearing again. It was good they disappeared, because most of them smelled like old mothballs and liked to pinch my cheeks until they hurt. That's another reason I love Uncle Lenny. He's never, ever pinched my cheeks or smelled like mothballs. He smells like warm bread most of the time, and freshly baked cookies some of the time.

He's a taxi driver and only works at night. He loves his job and tells us the funniest stories about all the different kinds of people who have jumped into the back of his car. Like the time a famous actress got in and ordered him to drive around for a whole hour just so she could get some sleep. Or the time a large Italian family spent the whole ride silently fighting over a single portion of fish and chips.

Whenever my Uncle Lenny visits us, he always brings a large bag of food shopping – and a chocolate bar just for me. He doesn't usually come with my Aunt Christina, because she doesn't like us. I don't know why. But it's OK because I don't like her either. She's very beautiful and is always perfectly dressed with perfect hair and with perfect make-up on her face. But she wrinkles up her nose whenever she sees something she doesn't like – which is nearly all the time, so she always looks as if she's smelled a bag of bad eggs. She has a fake smile too. It's one of those smiles that shows lots of teeth, but which never travels to any other part of her face. I don't trust people who can't smile with their whole face. It means they're trying to hide something from you. Fake smiles always make me want to get as far away from the Fake Smiler as possible.

Their son Jacob is OK. But he's only two and likes to break things, so I try to hide all my best toys from him when he comes over. After I finished setting up the Scrabble board, I helped Mum tidy up the house and was making my bedsheets extra straight when the doorbell rang.

'All right, all right, all right! How's my favourite nearly-ten-year-old doing?' shouted Uncle Lenny when I opened the door. He always says that, even though I know I'm the only nearly-ten-year-old he knows, which means he can't have any other favourites.

'OK.' I shrugged.

'Only OK?' he asked, bending down and looking

me in the eyes. 'Hmm! Might need to send you to the Smile Doctor.'

I smiled wider.

'That's better!' He ruffled my hair and gave me a kiss on the cheek, then heaved two large grocery bags into the kitchen.

'Afternoon!' said my Aunt Christina. Her lips were pinched together, and she was wearing so much perfume that it made my nose tickle.

'Jacob's asleep, so you'll have to play with him later!' she said matter-of-factly, as she carried Jacob in through the door and stuck out her pointy face at me. I stood on my tiptoes and gave her a kiss. She pulled away quickly.

'Right! What have you been up to then?' asked Uncle Lenny, as he came and steered me to the kitchen table. I think he must be so used to driving his taxi that he liked to drive people around too.

'Nothing!' I shrugged. 'Do you want to play Scrabble with me now, Uncle Lenny?'

'We'll have a game after lunch, my little tiger,' he smiled. 'I'm not on until five today!'

'Darling, why don't you tell Uncle Lenny all about your new friend?' asked Mum as she set the table.

'Oh yeah! The pomegranate boy!' said Uncle Lenny. 'Your mum told me. What's happening there then?'

'Lots!' I said. I began to tell him all about The Big Fight and The Mysterious Plant Pot Murder and The Great Baked Beans Bag Trap and Ahmet's story. And as we ate our lunch, I told them all about the bombs and the fires and the orange boat and the tents and Ahmet's cat and the railway track and the wall with the barbed wire on it.

Uncle Lenny shook his head and muttered 'Poor tyke!' every few minutes, and Mum nodded along looking sad sometimes, but Aunt Christina looked bored. Then, just as I was about to tell them about my new list of questions, Aunt Christina said, 'Doesn't surprise me you would want to be friends with a refugee kid at all, sweetheart. You'd have lots of things in common with him. What with your Gran having been a refugee too.'

Uncle Lenny and Mum looked up sharply.

'I can't even bear to think about it . . . Imagine! Being a war refugee back in the day? Before they all got loads of benefits and houses nicer than our ones . . .'

Uncle Lenny looked up angrily and was about to say something, when, just then, Jacob began to cry.

Aunt Christina jumped up and with a sniff, said, 'Oh dear, seems he's christened the nappy again!' before rushing out of the room.

'Mum, is that true?' I asked, looking at Mum so hard that it felt like my eyes were about to pop out of my head. 'Was Gran a refugee too?'

'All yours,' muttered Uncle Lenny, as he got up and walked over to one of the shopping bags. 'I'll get dessert, shall I?'

Mum looked at me for a moment, and then she said, 'Yes sweetheart, it is. Your Grandma Jo. We went to see her with Daddy when you were little. Do you remember her?'

I nodded. Not because I really remembered anything, but because I had looked at all the photographs hundreds of times. I was five, and it was the last time my mum and dad and me went on holiday in a real-life plane. We went to a town called Salzburg, which is in a country called Austria, because that's where Dad lived before he moved to England. He used to talk about the mountains and the rivers and the way the birds always seemed to follow him around. He looked so happy in all the photographs. So did Mum.

I seemed to be crying in most of my photos, so I'm not sure if I was happy or not. I don't really remember anything about the trip except for the large green wooden caravan my Grandma Jo had in her back garden. Dad used to sleep in it in the summer holidays when he was a boy. My grandad had built it before he died, which is why Dad wanted to become a carpenter. There's a photo of me and Dad sitting on its steps and it's the only photo of me where I'm not crying. Even then I must have liked the idea of sleeping in a bright green caravan.

I couldn't really remember anything about my Grandma Jo. But we had lots and lots of photos of her and Dad, and I always look at them whenever I miss Dad too much.

She had short grey hair and wore glasses that were tied to a long golden chain, and she always wore flowery tops and white trousers. I wished I could have remembered her more, but sometimes no matter how hard you try or how badly you might want to, your brain can't reach that far back.

'Why was she a refugee?' I asked. 'Did she run away from bombs like Ahmet?'

Mum stayed quiet as Uncle Lenny placed four large chocolate éclairs on the table in front of us. I love chocolate éclairs because it's like having three desserts in one. But as much as I wanted to eat my éclair, I wanted to hear the answers to my questions more.

Uncle Lenny sat back down and cleared his throat. 'Don't think they've done World War Two in school yet have they?' he asked my mum quietly.

Mum shook her head.

'World War *Two*?' I asked. 'You mean there was another one?'

Uncle Lenny nodded. 'Yup. Just like the one you learnt about last year, but twice as bad!' he whispered, as though it was a secret.

Mum put my éclair on a plate and pushed it towards me. 'All you need to know, darling, is that Grandma Jo was a wonderful person, and that she helped lots of refugees just like your friend Ahmet run away from a war too,' she said.

'Were they running away from Syria as well?' I asked, wondering just how long a war lasted.

'No, darling,' said Mum, putting her own éclair on a plate. 'They ran away from a different war. One that started in Germany, and they were running away from people who called themselves Nazis.'

'Oh,' I said, wondering just how many wars I needed to learn about.

'Anyway, the important thing is she survived! And she got to see *you*,' exclaimed Uncle Lenny, as he gave my hair a stroke.

'Exactly,' said Mum, tapping my hand. 'Now, eat up, and let's get a game of Scrabble going before Uncle Lenny has to leave!'

I nodded, and, knowing that my mum didn't want me to ask any more questions, broke open my éclair.

That afternoon, Uncle Lenny stayed and played two whole games of Scrabble with us, and Aunt Christina watched Jacob break one of Mum's vases, rip a book, and throw my Lego bricks across the room. Mum won the first game and Uncle Lenny won the second one, and I got the lowest points I had ever gotten in history. But I didn't mind. I don't think you can really focus on playing a game when you've just found out that your grandma was a refugee, who had helped lots of other refugees run away from a war too. Even if you're playing a game that's as fun as Scrabble.

SYRAH AND THE SEA

When we all got to school that first Monday of the second term, it turned out that nearly everyone had heard of Ahmet's story. It had spread over the holiday more quickly than news of a new flavoured packet of crisps, and just as quickly as he had become famous for being 'The Boy that Beat Brendan-the-Bully', Ahmet became famous for being 'That Refugee Boy'.

I don't think anyone kept their promise to Mrs Khan of not asking him any questions, because everyone in class tried to sneak in at least one whenever they talked to him. Even Josie and Michael and Tom couldn't help themselves and started to ask him things like, 'Did you have cheese sandwiches in Syria?' or 'What was the weather like in Greece?' or 'Did you ever eat snails and frogs in France?' I don't think Ahmet minded because we were his friends. If he understood the question, he would just answer 'yes' or 'no', and if he didn't understand he would just stare at us or shrug. But there were lots of people he didn't know asking him lots of questions too. Some of them asked so many questions in one go that even we couldn't understand what they were saying – and we could speak English!

Some classes even began to send Messengers to see if they could find anything out. Messengers are usually the smallest kids in a class, and are paid in sweets or football stickers or extra lunch tokens to get information. Some of them are OK and leave you alone if you tell them that you don't want to say anything. But the ones that work for the school bullies are especially annoying. It's not their fault really, because they get beaten up if they go back with nothing new to tell, but sometimes they won't listen to you even after you've already given them an answer. The most annoying Messenger in school is Victor.

Victor's extra skinny, even though he eats chips every day, and he has a gold earring in his ear. He works for two upper school bullies whose names I don't know, but who always hang around the lower boys' toilets and shake anyone that goes in until everything falls out of their pockets. But he also works for a group of girls who always stand around the water fountain, so you never really know who he's Messenger-ing for.

After everyone had found out Ahmet was a refugee, Victor followed us around for nearly a whole week. At break-times, at lunch-times and even at home-times, he would suddenly appear and ask lots of questions that even I found strange. Like, 'Where did you get your shoes from?', 'Are you scared of fireworks?', 'Can you make a tent from a shirt?' and 'Are you really nine or are you secretly older?'

He got so annoying that even the break-duty teachers began to notice and told him to leave Ahmet alone. Except Mr Irons. He was the only teacher who didn't say anything. After he got told off by Mrs Sanders and Ms Hemsi one break, Victor stayed away, but his questions stayed with us. Sometimes words hang around longer than people, even when you don't want them to. And whenever I was on my own or just with Tom and Josie and Michael, Victor's questions would pop up into my head and make me wonder what they meant.

The only thing that was even more annoying than the Messengers was Brendan-the-Bully. Because instead of being nicer to Ahmet after seeing his pictures and hearing his story, Brendan-the-Bully became even more horrible. He seemed to have forgotten that Ahmet could turn into a lion and punch him hundreds of times, because he began to whisper, 'Oi! Smelly Refuge Bag!' whenever he saw him, and in class, he would throw spit-balls whenever Mrs Khan or Ms Hemsi weren't looking. When we told Ahmet to tell Mrs Khan or Mrs Sanders about it, he shook his head and said, 'I not scared. Lots of badder people in camps. My dad say I fight them. So, I fight him.'

When Ahmet said this, I thought he was very brave, so on Halloween, I brought in one of my favourite Tintin books for him to look at – because in it, Tintin stays and fights lots of bad guys, even though the bad guys are bigger and there are lots more of them. There are *always* lots more of them!

'See. You! You're like this! See?' I said, showing him the book. I was dressed as a vampire and Ahmet was dressed as a green monster – although Tom said it was the Hulk. We were sitting in the playground on our own because Tom and Josie and Michael were still eating their lunch and taking too long.

'Tintin!' he cried out, when he saw the cover.

'You know Tintin?' I asked, surprised. I hadn't thought about it before, but I guess Tintin really is famous everywhere!

'Yes!' said Ahmet. 'I read all time. My dad – he read them to me.'

I nodded, remembering the voices my dad used to make when he read the comics to me too. After a while, I said, 'I have all of them. You can see them if you like.'

'I keep this?' asked Ahmet.

'Oh,' I said. I hadn't really meant to give him the book – I had only wanted to show it to him. But I knew I could ask Mum to find me another old copy in the library and save it for me when it was about to be thrown away, so I shrugged and said, 'Sure!'

Ahmet gave me a big smile and started to flick through it. He stopped at a page and pointed at Captain Haddock. 'My dad . . . he had this,' he said, moving his finger so that it pointed to Captain Haddock's beard. 'You?'

I shook my head. 'No, my dad didn't have a beard. But also . . . my dad . . . he's dead . . .'

Ahmet nodded sadly and looked down at the picture. 'I not know where is Dad. Maybe he dead too.'

I looked over at Ahmet. 'He's not here in London?' I asked.

Ahmet shook his head. 'I come here. My dad . . . he behind.'

I frowned. 'Behind? Where?'

Ahmet shrugged and looked down at the comic book. 'Maybe he in France.'

'Oh,' I said, feeling sad for him. I'd hate it if I didn't know where my dad was or if he was still alive. I wanted to ask who the lady in the red scarf was, and whether she could help him find his dad. And where his mum and his sister and his cat were. But then Ahmet flicked to another page and held it up to me. He was pointing to a picture. In it, Tintin and Captain Haddock and Snowy and a man with an eye-patch were all standing on a raft in the middle of the ocean, and Captain Haddock was waving a flag that had been made out of his blue jumper.

'Sea . . .' said Ahmet, quietly.

I nodded.

'I have sister,' he said. 'She there now.'

'You mean here?' I asked, pointing to the raft.

'No,' said Ahmet. 'Here.' He pointed to the ocean.

And then I understood.

'Oh,' I said. I felt strange – as if something had just hit me on the inside of my chest. It was the same feeling I had in the hospital when Mum and Uncle Lenny told me that Dad had died.

'You mean . . . your sister . . .'

'Her name Syrah,' said Ahmet.

'Syrah . . . she is . . . *in* the sea?'

Ahmet nodded and rubbed his eyes.

'Then she's not with your cat?' I asked quietly.

Ahmet shook his head. 'Cat dead . . . in mountains.' And then, flicking to another page, he pointed to a tent and said, 'Mum sick. Last time I see her.'

'Oh,' I said. I wanted to cry, but Ahmet wasn't crying so I didn't think I should either. Instead I stared at the picture he was pointing to just as hard as I could so that he couldn't see my eyes.

We didn't say anything else after that, because a few seconds later, Michael and Josie came out and joined us. Tom was still inside because it was chocolate pudding day and he always tried to get an extra piece after everyone else had left. I waited to see if Ahmet would show them the pictures and tell them about Syrah and the sea and his mum too. But he didn't, and when he looked at me and shook his head, I knew that he wanted me to keep it a secret.

I nodded back and made a silent promise to Ahmet that I wouldn't tell anyone. But I didn't know that I would be forced to break my promise the very next day. Because that was when I heard Something. And it was a Something so scary, that it changed Everything.

13

THE SOMETHING THAT CHANGED EVERYTHING

The night after Ahmet had told me about his sister Syrah being in the sea and not knowing if his mum and dad were alive, I had trouble getting to sleep. My mum always tells me to count sheep when I can't sleep. But I find sheep too funny – they look like clouds with legs – so I count leopards instead. They're colourful and look serious. I can't remember how many leopards I counted to, but it must have been more than two hundred before I eventually drifted off.

By the time the morning arrived, I was so tired, and my legs moved so slowly, that when I got to the bus stop it was late, and Tom and Josie and Michael had already left. I didn't really mind, because getting the bus on my own is fun. I like watching the people passing by on the streets outside, or making guesses about the people sitting next to me. Last week, there was a huge man sitting right at the front of the bus, snoring so loudly that he was making all the windows shake. Everyone was watching him and giggling or shaking their heads at him. But what if he had been a world-famous snorer on his way to the International Snoring Championships and was practising his best snore? You just never know.

That morning, I was too sleepy to look at anyone and guess stories about them, so I leaned my head on the large window and listened instead. There are always lots of noises on a bus – especially when there are lots of people going to work and trying to get to school – but it's usually noises like the doors opening and closing, and people ringing the bell, and tickets beeping on the ticket machine. Nobody really talks to anyone else, unless they're with friends or asking for a seat. Uncle Lenny says it's because we're English, and English people would rather die than have to speak to someone they don't know. I think I can't be very English, if that's true.

The bus had passed two stops and except for a baby who was making loud gurgling noises, it was nice and quiet. I think everyone must have been as sleepy as me.

But then at the third stop, a woman dressed in a bright yellow coat, and a man dressed in a suit, came and sat in front of me and, picking up the free newspaper lying on both their seats, began talking loudly about all the things they were reading.

At first, they talked about the Economy being broken by rich people who weren't paying their taxes and hiding all their money away in a place called Off Shore. Then they talked about a princess who was going out with an actor they didn't like and a famous singer who had been arrested for hitting someone. I was starting to fall asleep again when the man suddenly said something which made me sit up in my seat and listen just as hard as I could.

'Oh, ain't it horrible,' the man said. 'Look at what they're saying about refugees! Border restrictions as of next month . . . I knew this would happen.'

The woman shook her head, looking over his shoulder at the paper. 'Those poor people. Where are they meant to go? Back to that nightmare they left behind, or left to starve in France?'

'Cheaper for us to leave them in France,' said the man, shaking his head. 'Says here the borders will be closed by the end of the month. So that's all the racists made happy then!'

The woman tutted. 'Rescuing kids out of the sea one minute, and then telling them they can't be helped the next! Some of them might have family here, poor things. That should count for something.'

The man read the newspaper for a few more seconds and then said, 'Well, apparently not. Says here we've already taken in a few hundred, so we're not going take in any more. Doesn't matter how little they are.'

It was my stop. As soon as I got off the bus, I ran as fast as I could to school. My heart was beating so loudly that I could hear it in my ears, but I didn't care. If what the man said was right, then after next month Ahmet's mum and dad would never be allowed into England – and Ahmet would never see them again. I needed to tell Tom and Michael and Josie about what I had just heard. And I had to tell them everything without Ahmet hearing!

But when I reached the school gates, the bell for registration was already ringing and the playground was nearly empty. I ran to the classroom just before

Mrs Khan started to take the register. She looked at me with a frown but didn't say anything.

'Where were you?' whispered Josie. 'We waited until the second bus came!'

I was too out of breath to say lots of words, so I just said, 'Slept . . . late.'

That morning, Mrs Khan put us into two big groups so that we could write a play on the story of Romulus and Remus and then act it out. It's a legend about two baby boys whose mum hid them in a basket and sent them far away so that they wouldn't be killed by people who were jealous of them. I guess they were Refugee Boys like Ahmet was, except Ahmet's mum didn't put him in a basket. He came in a boat.

Mrs Khan and Ms Hemsi said Ahmet could join the class on this project, so Ahmet and Tom were put in my group, and Michael and Josie were put in the other group. I was trying to think of how to let them know of what I'd heard, when Mrs Khan told everyone to get a piece of coloured paper and a special handwriting pen from her desk so that we could write out our own lines. I decided to take an extra piece of paper, and while everyone was busy looking through their workbooks to find out which character they wanted to play, I quickly wrote a Top-Secret Message.

It said this:

> I heard something on the bus!
> We musn't tell Ahmet about it!
> Meet me in the library at break-time.
> TOP SECRET.

I folded the Message up until it was so small that I could hide it in my hand, and when Mrs Khan and Ms Hemsi weren't looking, I passed it to Tom. Tom looked around and when nobody except me was watching him, he opened it up and read it. Then he gave me a nod, and pretending to need another piece of paper, went up to Mrs Khan's desk and gave Josie the note on the way back to his seat. Then I saw Josie read the note and quickly pass it to Michael – who dropped it on the floor. But luckily, everyone was too busy writing their lines to notice and he snatched it back up again. He looked over at me and gave me a thumbs-up, and then stuffed the Top-Secret Message into his pocket.

As soon as the bell for first break began to ring and Mrs Khan told us to leave everything where it was, I ran to the library room and waited outside. It was the one place in school no one ever tried to go into at break-time. A few minutes later, Josie and Michael came running up the corridor.

'Tom's in the playground with Ahmet,' said Josie. 'We can fill him in later.'

'What did you hear?' asked Michael, his eyes wide.

I quickly told them everything that the man and woman on the bus had said, about no more refugees being allowed into the country, and then what Ahmet had told me about his mum and dad being left behind. I had to tell them about his sister Syrah too. I felt bad about breaking my promise, but I knew that Ahmet wouldn't mind me telling Josie and Michael about it, because this was a real emergency and they were his friends too.

'You mean . . . if he doesn't find them before the end of the month, then Ahmet might never see his mum and dad again?' gasped Josie.

I shook my head. 'Not once the government closes the border gates!'

'Yeah,' said Michael. 'They're like giant airport ones with loads of police and guards protecting them – and you can't go through them when they're closed or you get put in jail.' Michael looked at his watch and pressed a button so that it lit up and showed the date. 'If they're closing all the gates at the end of this month ... that means he's only got nine days to find them!'

'What do we do?' asked Josie.

'I say we tell Mrs Khan and Ms Hemsi – they'll know what to do!' I said.

Michael and Josie agreed. We ran to the staff room and knocked loudly on the door. We're not supposed to disturb teachers in the staff room at break-time, because that's where they go to drink lots of tea and find answers to questions that they can't find in their answer-books. I know because Josie's aunt is a teacher, and she told Josie, who told me. But Mrs Khan and Ms Hemsi had told us to go and find them if Something was wrong. And this Something felt like the most wrong Something I had ever heard of.

After a few seconds, Mr Gaffer opened the door and looked down at us with a frown. He's the Deputy

Head, which means he's in charge on the days Mrs Sanders is away. But Mrs Sanders is never ever away, so I don't really know what he does.

'Yes?' he asked.

'Please sir – we need to see Mrs Khan and Ms Hemsi IMMEDIATELY,' I said.

'It's an EMERGENCY!' added Josie.

'Is it really?' he said suspiciously.

We all nodded our heads at least ten times.

'All right – just hold on . . .' replied Mr Gaffer, as he closed the door.

Josie twisted her hair nervously around her finger and stuffed a whole chunk in her mouth, and Michael started kicking the wall lightly as we waited. After what felt like twenty whole minutes but couldn't really have been more than one, Mrs Khan and Ms Hemsi came to the door.

'Is something the matter?' asked Mrs Khan. 'Is it to do with Ahmet?'

We all nodded again.

Ms Hemsi and Mrs Khan stepped out into the corridor and closed the staff room door behind them. We all started talking at once.

Mrs Khan held up her hands and said, 'Calm down, calm down! Now. One at a time please.'

'Miss, the government are going to close the gates!' I began.

Josie said, 'And Ahmet's mum and dad are on the other side. They might get stuck!'

'And there's only nine days left until the gates close,' said Michael, showing Mrs Khan his watch.'

Mrs Khan and Ms Hemsi looked at each other and then looked back at us.

'What do you mean by "gates"?' asked Mrs Khan gently.

'You know – the gates at the edge of the borders!' said Michael. 'The ones where all the police with the big guns are. The refugees have to come through them to get into the country.'

'Ah,' said Mrs Khan. 'And where did you hear they were going to be closed? Was it on the news?'

I told her about the man and woman on the bus.

'I see,' said Mrs Khan. She was quiet for a moment, and I saw her give Ms Hemsi another look. Then she said, 'Ahmet is a lucky boy to have such caring friends. But you don't have to worry at all. His foster mother, who you've seen coming to pick him up every single day after school, is there to look after him, until his family can be found, and she's working with some very clever people to try and help Ahmet find his family just as quickly as possible.'

We all looked over at each other in surprise. So the woman in the red scarf was Ahmet's foster mum! Everything was beginning to make sense and all our questions were being answered too.

'Clever people like who, Miss?' asked Michael.

'Well, clever people from the government,' said Mrs Khan.

'And lawyers and some wonderful kind-hearted Ministers who are working in Parliament, and charities too,' said Ms Hemsi.

'That's right,' agreed Mrs Khan. 'They're doing everything they can to make sure Ahmet's mum and dad are found. That's their job.'

'But . . . what if they don't find his family before they close the gates?' I asked.

Ms Hemsi and Mrs Khan smiled, but they didn't smile with their whole faces, so I knew right away that they were just pretend smiles.

'Everyone is doing everything they can,' said Mrs Khan again.

Ms Hemsi nodded, and then looking at me, asked, 'Ahmet spoke to you about his family ... and what happened to his sister?'

I nodded, but suddenly felt nervous. I had promised Ahmet that I would keep it a secret and I hadn't.

Ms Hemsi smiled, and said my name softly. 'That's a very good thing,' she said. 'A very, *very* good thing.'

The bell rang, and Mrs Khan made us promise not to upset Ahmet by talking about the border gates, or telling anyone else about his sister. We all promised, and Mrs Khan said, 'Everything will be fine. You'll see.'

I nodded, but I didn't think she sounded very sure. In fact, I didn't think everything was going to be fine at all. Not if Ahmet didn't find his family before the gates closed!

That afternoon we told Tom what had happened and we all came to a decision. We were going to try and help instead.

And to do that, we would need to go on our First Ever Top Secret Mission.

THE THREE PLANS

In the movies, people who go on a Top Secret Mission always have lots of fun gadgets and maps and ropes and sometimes even wear a cool hat. When you're nine-and-over-three-quarters, though, and have to go to school every day, rescue missions are a lot harder – especially when you don't know where the people you want to rescue are, and you have to hide everything you're doing from the person you're going on the mission for.

But even though we didn't have any gadgets or ropes or hats, we spent every break-time and lunch-time and home-time trying to think up new ideas that might help Ahmet find his family quickly. By Thursday morning, Tom and Josie and Michael had each come up with a plan. But I hadn't been able to think of anything.

'Don't worry,' said Josie. 'You can help us see if our ones will work.'

I tried to smile but it didn't make me feel any better.

On the way to school we went through all the plans. Tom went first. He said we should write to the Prime Minister to tell her to keep the gates open until Ahmet had found his family. He had even gotten the address of the Prime Minister's house from his dad and written out the letter.

This is what it looked like:

Dear Prime Minster,

We heard from some peeple on the bus that the Goverment was going to lock the gates so that no more Refujees could come in. But our friend Ahmet is a refujee boy — you might have heard about him becaus he's famuos for beating up Brendan The Bully and he doesn't know where his mum and dad are and needs to find them. Please Prime Minster can you please keep the gates open so that he can find them and so that he can be happy again.

Thank you.

I thought it was a good idea and so did Josie, but Michael said it wouldn't work because the Prime Minister was in charge of the government and had probably been the one who told the security guards to lock the gates and sent them her special keys. So we couldn't ask her for any help at all.

Then Josie talked about her plan which was called the Special Appeal. She said we should ring a newspaper and tell them all about it, because her mum and dad were always complaining about how many Special Appeals there were for charities in their newspapers. And once the appeal went out, Ahmet's mum and dad would see it and get in touch. Josie had written the Special Appeal out and made it as short as possible so that the newspapers could print it quickly.

This is what it looked like:

SPESCHAL APPEAL

Please every1, a boy called Ahmet
who is in Nelson School ran away
from Syria becoase of bombs and
lost his mum and dad 2. If you C a
man and a woman who looks like
this is their son or your Ahmet's

Picture of
Ahmet

mum and dad please ring Mrs Khan on the telephone
number at our school which is below. We need to
find Ahmet's family before the gates are locked
which is Y this Appeal is So Speschal.

We all liked the Special Appeal plan, but then Tom said
that even if we did put the appeal in a newspaper, the
newspaper would only be sold in England and Ahmet's
mum and dad and anyone who might have seen them
would never see it. He knew, because when he lived in
America he only ever saw American newspapers, and that's
what it must be like in all the countries of the world too.

Then Michael told us about his plan. 'We should
write to the High Court, to the Judge sitting in the
highest chair in the land, and ask them to order all the

security guards to open the gates when they see Ahmet's mum and dad,' he whispered. 'It's called an Appeal too. I've heard my mum talking about them because her law firm are always doing them for people. I'd ask her to help Ahmet but she's always complaining about how much work she has to do *and* she charges hundreds of pounds an hour.'

'But we can't afford that!' cried out Tom.

'I know,' replied Michael, rolling his eyes. 'Which is why I'm saying we should do the appeal ourselves.'

'Is it an Appeal like my newspaper one?' asked Josie.

'Sort of. Except it's for a Judge. All we need to do is find out who the Highest Judge in the Land is and write to them!' replied Michael. 'We could even send them your Appeal,' he said, giving Josie a nudge on the arm. 'We'd only need to change it a little bit. Mum's always saying that Judges have nothing better to do than read Appeals all the time.'

We were all excited about this idea the most, and as no one could think of anything that might be wrong with it, we decided to go to the school library at home-time to find out the name of the Highest Judge in the

Land. So, when the last bell rang, we told Ahmet we had to get home quickly so he wouldn't follow us, and headed straight there.

Our school library isn't as big as the one Mum works in, but it has larger windows and lots more sunlight which means you can see all the books better. Mrs Finnicky is our Librarian. She always wears bright-coloured clothes and bright red lipstick, and you don't ever have to look for her because she's always standing behind the library counter.

I like Mrs Finnicky because she always gets excited when you ask her anything. She tells people off for not looking after their books properly, just like Mum. She has a large sign on the counter that says, 'Books are like people. Look past their covers, and they'll take you on a Great Adventure!' I like it because it's fun to imagine people as books and guess about what kind of adventure they might take you on.

When we got to the library counter, we all looked up at Mrs Finnicky – she was wearing a sky-blue top and a sky-blue skirt – and Mrs Finnicky smiled and looked down at all of us and said, 'Hello! And how can I help you all today?'

Tom and Josie and me all looked over at Michael and waited, so he asked, 'Miss, do you know where we can find out who the Highest Judge in the Land is? We need to find out . . . for . . . er . . . homework!'

'Really?' said Mrs Finnicky, frowning.

We all nodded. Mrs Finnicky scratched her chin. 'I think we'll have to look online for that,' she said, and she started typing into her computer.

We nodded and waited excitedly for an answer as Mrs Finnicky narrowed her eyes and looked at the screen. After a few seconds she said, 'Here we go . . . Right. Was it the name of the Lord Chief Justice you were after, or the High Court Judge for the Family Division?'

We all looked at each other and then Michael said, 'Family Division, please!'

Mrs Finnicky wrote the name out on a piece of paper. When she gave it to Michael, we all looked over his shoulder and read, 'HC Family Division, Dame Leslie Williamson.'

'Anything else?' asked Mrs Finnicky.

Josie said, 'Does it have her address there, Miss?'

Mrs Finnicky frowned again. 'Her address?' she

asked. 'You have to send her a letter as part of your homework?'

We all nodded.

'So that it gets to her by tomorrow,' I added.

'It's the High Court of Justice you'll be needing to write to,' said Mrs Finnicky, narrowing her eyes at the computer screen again as she copied it down. 'But even if you post it today and it gets to her office tomorrow or on Saturday, remember that the courts are closed over the weekend, and it won't be the judge who gets your envelope – she'll have a secretary to open her mail for her.' She handed the slip of paper with the address to Josie. 'Anything else?' She looked at our downcast faces. 'I'm sure she'll read your letter eventually,' she added gently. 'It might just take a while.'

We left and gathered in the hallway outside. 'What are we going to do now?' asked Josie. Her face was all pink, which is what happens when she's really upset. 'Even if we send the Judge that Appeal right away, the gates will be shut before she even gets it. It's already Thursday and after this weekend is over we'll only have five more days . . .'

160

We all looked at Michael, who shrugged and looked at the floor.

'We've *got* to think of another idea,' said Tom urgently.

We all nodded. But I felt sick inside. I was scared that Ahmet's family wouldn't be found in time.

We were all silent on the bus ride home that afternoon. Everyone was thinking, hard, but I could tell from all our faces that none of us had come up with anything.

I felt the worst, because at least everyone else had thought of something. I hadn't come up with a single plan. Now I know it was because my brain just wasn't ready to think of anything then. It wouldn't be ready until the weekend, but when it was, it came up with a plan so fantastic that nobody could say no to it. Not even a Judge sitting in the Highest Chair in the Land.

15

THE GREATEST IDEA IN THE WORLD

That Thursday night, while Mum was at work, instead of doing my homework, I took my Tintin pencil case and my exercise book and went and sat down by the window in the kitchen.

I wanted to come up with a plan just like Tom and Josie and Michael had done, and thought that if I sat there, maybe my brain would come up with something exciting all on its own. I have a desk in my room, but I like sitting in the kitchen more because then I can see the sky and the whole city too. Tom says it doesn't matter how big or small a flat is, if it's on the top floor it becomes a Pent House. That's a kind of house that movie stars live in. I guess they must like sitting in kitchens and looking at skies and cities too.

I waited a long time for my brain to think of something, but when Mum came home she found me still sitting at the kitchen table, pressing the Snowy and Captain Haddock buttons on my pencil case. I couldn't think of anything, not even after she came and sat with me to watch the sunset. I love watching the sunset with Mum. She calls it the 'Magic Hour' because you can see colours you won't ever see again and birds that might fly away for ever, swimming across the skies together. But I can only ever do it properly with Mum. I've tried to watch the sunset on my own and feel just as happy, but I can't seem to do it at all. It doesn't work.

By dinner-time, I still hadn't thought of anything, so I went straight to bed to see if my brain could think of things better when it was lying down. But I fell asleep instead, and had a nightmare that was so scary it made me wake up. I had dreamt of being on a piece of wood in the middle of a dark sea. At first it had been quiet, but then to my right, a girl had begun to cry – she was about to be swallowed by a giant whale, and suddenly on my left, my dad was shouting for help from a sinking boat. And no matter how hard I tried or how much I wanted to, I couldn't help the girl or stop my dad from disappearing into the water.

If you've ever woken up after a nightmare when it's pitch black and so late that nothing in the world is awake, you'll know it isn't nice at all. When I woke up, I couldn't hear anything or see anything, so for a moment I wasn't sure if I was awake or still in my nightmare. But then I heard one of the mice squeaking in the kitchen and I knew I was awake.

That's a good thing about animals. They always let you know they're around. Especially when they're hungry. And if they're around, then you know you're real and the world around you is real too.

I was feeling hot and damp so I got up and pulled back the covers to make sure I hadn't wet the bed. Luckily, I hadn't. I hate wetting the bed. I used to do it all the time after Dad died, but then, when I turned seven, something happened, and I stopped doing it. Maybe when you turn seven, your body knows you've become too old to wet the bed any more.

I didn't want to lie back down in case I had the

nightmare again, so I tiptoed into the kitchen to get a glass of water and see the mice. Mum says that years ago, an old woman who bred all sorts of exotic animals used to live in our flat. That could be why we found a small nest of bright yellow snakes in our kitchen wall last summer. Or why we have two mice living with us. But I don't mind. I like mice because they make good friends. For just a tiny piece of food, they can become your friends for life. They disappear if they don't like you, so you always know if they're going to be your friends right from the start. And it's always good to know from the start because it saves you from wasting your best cheese.

After I got a drink of water, I went back to my room. But I was still too scared to go back to sleep, so I sat on the floor and got one of my favourite Tintin comics out from underneath my bed. It was the one about a rich old opera singer who comes to stay with Captain Haddock – even though he really doesn't want her to – and whose green diamond gets stolen. I couldn't really concentrate on the story because all I could think about was Ahmet and his sister Syrah being in the sea. But then, just as I was thinking how the rich old opera singer looked like the Queen – except with a much bigger nose – it suddenly happened!

I had it!

An idea!

And it was without a doubt, quite possibly, the Greatest Idea in the World! It leapt right into my head, just like a giant frog, and jumped around until I knew it had to work! It just had to!

You can always tell when you've had a Greatest Idea in the World because it pops up from nowhere. Ordinary ideas take an awfully long time to become an idea because they're ordinary, so your brain can't get excited about them and has to make them slowly – like thousands of boring bread rolls being baked in an extra slow oven. But when an idea is truly great, it doesn't take any time at all – it just suddenly appears and makes your eyes go wide and your brain feel as if it's just been pushed out of bed.

Jumping to my feet, I got out my exercise book and drew out my plan. This is what the Greatest Idea in the World looked like:

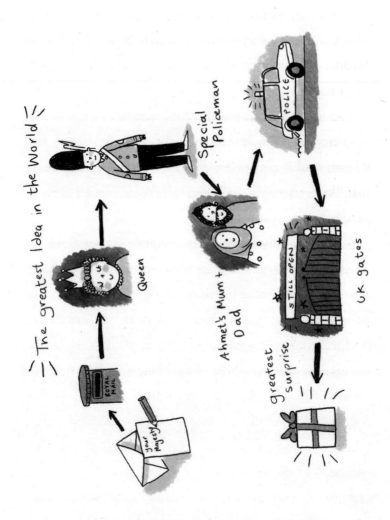

The greatest Idea in the World

Queen

Special Policeman

Ahmet's Mum + Dad

POLICE

STILL OPEN

UK gates

Your majesty

ROYAL MAIL

greatest surprise

167

When I had finished, I stared at it and went over it again and again in my head. I knew right away that it would work – but only if Tom and Josie and Michael helped and kept it all a secret. I got back into bed and lay there, wishing for the morning to come. Because as soon as it did, I was going to put the Greatest Idea in the World into action and help Ahmet find his family.

I knew it was going to be the most exciting thing any of us had ever done and that there was a chance it might get us into trouble too.

What I didn't know was just how dangerous an adventure it was going to be – and quite *how* much trouble it was going to get us in . . .

THE ROYAL LETTER

'It's brilliant!'

'Genius!'

'If that doesn't work then nothing will!'

Michael, Tom and Josie all looked pretty impressed when I explained the Greatest Idea in the World to them on the bus to school the next day.

Tom looked down at my diagram and eagerly pointed to the letter and pencil. 'This bit's easy,' he said. 'But do you think she'll really get it?'

I nodded. 'She has to. It's the *Royal* Mail – so she *has* to get all her letters. It's the law.'

'But she's the *Queen*. What if she's not home cos she's somewhere else doing her duties and things and doesn't get it in time?' asked Michael. 'It's already Friday, remember.'

Michael was right; the Greatest Idea in the World would only work if the Queen was at home. She was always on the news going to lots of places to collect flowers from people. And I hadn't thought about what we would do if she didn't get the letter at all . . .

'It's OK,' said Josie reassuringly. 'If we post the letter today, then it'll get to her house by tomorrow morning. Tomorrow's only Saturday – and the gates don't close until next Friday. That gives us six whole days. So, if she's *not* home, her butler will just open the letter instead, and *he'll* let her know that she needs to come home right away to talk to the special police and the Prime Minister!'

'Yesssss!' said Michael. 'Exactly!'

'Yeah. It's going to be brilliant,' said Tom, as we jumped off the bus and walked to the school gates. 'There's no WAY she won't help us. Not after she reads about Ahmet.'

'But he mustn't find out,' said Michael, tripping over his shoelaces but too excited to stop and tie them up.

'Yeah.' I nodded. 'He can't know – not until we're really sure that the Queen has found his parents.'

'Don't worry – we can keep it a secret. And maybe if it does work, then we'll all get to meet the Queen!' grinned Tom. 'I'll have to get more gel if we do . . .' he added, stiffening his hair with his fingers so that it was spikier than ever.

'Maybe we'll all get a medal for helping to keep the gates open!' said Josie, kicking her football along. 'And Ahmet too – for being so brave.'

Michael smiled. His smile always goes to one side when he's thinking about something that makes him really, really happy. It must be because he's so happy that his mouth doesn't know which way to go. 'Yeah . . .' He nodded. 'One of those star-shaped medals. And if we did get one, we could pin it to our jumpers every day. Or if it's on a ribbon, we could wear it around our necks!' he said, touching the collar of his school jumper.

I tried to imagine what it would be like to meet the Queen and be given a star-shaped medal. But the thought made my mind go blank and I couldn't imagine anything at all. Sometimes a thought is so big that it can't squeeze all of itself into my head no matter how hard I try, and the more I try, the more it makes my head ache.

Uncle Lenny says that's where Head Aches all come from – when you've tried to think too many thoughts, or a giant thought tries to get in but it's too big to fit. He gets Head Aches all the time, because he says when there's no one in the taxi with him, he doesn't have anything else to do but drive around all night and think deep thoughts that light up his mind. Maybe that's why the front of his head is always so shiny. I didn't want to get a Head Ache, so I left the thought of the star-shaped medal alone.

All that day, whenever we knew Ahmet couldn't hear us, we talked about the Greatest Idea in the World and all the ways the Queen might help him and his family too. Ahmet caught us whispering together in the playground though, and looked at us in a confused way.

'What are you saying?' he asked, looking at all of us.

'Nothing!' said Michael, nervously.

'We were just talking about homework,' said Josie.

'Big homework,' I added, quickly crossing my fingers behind my back. 'Your homework is small – and easy, see? And ours is big and lots, lots more.'

'OK . . .' Ahmet said slowly, but I didn't think he sounded like he believed us.

After that we all whispered an agreement not to speak about the plan until home-time, which was when we planned to write the Royal Letter. But it seemed that the more excited we got about putting the Greatest Idea in the World into action, the longer it took for the day to pass. And that afternoon felt like the longest afternoon any of us had ever had.

I kept looking up at the classroom clock to see if its hands had moved and I could see Tom and Michael and Josie doing the same thing. Then finally, just as we were about to give up hope of them ever reaching quarter past three, the school bell rang for home-time and Mrs Khan said, 'Right, everyone, off you go. See you all on Monday!'

We all hurriedly waved bye to Ahmet, and, instead of going with him to meet his foster mum like we usually did, we ran to the bus stop just as fast as we could.

There's a wall behind the bus stop just long enough to fit five people. After we all sat down, Josie gave me a piece of yellow paper she had taken from her class tray and which was brand new, and Tom gave me his very best handwriting pen to use, and Michael gave me his workbook to lean on. He guessed we would have to miss two buses home. But it didn't matter. Not when we were trying to write the most Royal Letter any of us had ever written before!

Everyone said I should write it because I was the best at spelling. I was pretty nervous. But Tom and Josie and Michael all helped me choose what to say, so in the end, it wasn't as hard as I thought it was going to be.

This is what the Royal Letter looked like:

Your Royal Majesty of the United Queendom of England,

Please Mrs Majesty. There is a new boy in our class called Ahmet and he's a Refugee Boy from Syria where there is a War and lots of bullies throwing bombs and hurting people. Ahmet had to get on a boat and walked a long way to come to our school, and had to leave his Mum and Dad behind in tents too. Ahmet needs to find them before the Government closes all the gates.

We thought because you own the country and the police and the Prime Minister has to listen to you, that you could please ask your Special Police and the Prime Minister to keep all the gates open and help Ahmet find his family. We know the gates will close on Friday so this is an EMERJENCY.

You can find us at Nelson Primary School and Mrs Khan is our teacher and Ms Hemsi is Ahmet's Special Teacher.

Please let us know if you can help as soon as you get this letter.

Love from Me (9 and ¾), Tom (9), Michael (9 ½) And Josie (9 and ¼)

When we had finished, Michael held it up to the light and gave it a nod. I don't really know why people like holding things up to the light, but I guess it's because they want to see through them and make sure they're OK. I was glad because even though my writing had gone wonky, everyone said it looked good. It was the longest letter I had ever written in one go and my hand felt sore, so I jumped off the wall and jiggled it about. In the distance, I could see the bus coming.

'Have you got a new envelope to put it in? And stamps?' asked Tom anxiously, as we got onto the bus.

'Yup! Mum's got loads,' I said. 'And I'll post it by five o'clock from the post box in front of my flat.'

'Don't forget to write "Special Letter" on the envelope – in purple colouring pen,' said Josie. 'Purple's her favourite colour!'

'And make sure the stamp says "First" on it!' said Michael.

When I got home that afternoon, while Mrs Abbey was making me fish fingers for my tea, I quietly pulled open the big top drawer in the large chest standing in our living room. This drawer is called our 'Used-Less Things Drawer', because it's always full of things we have lots of, but hardly ever use – like paperclips and spare staples and elastic bands and Sellotape and bright yellow Post-it notes and bits of blank paper.

I found an envelope and then carefully took out Mum's small wooden stamp box. Inside it are all the Nearly-New Stamps that Mum's collected from letters she's been sent in the post. Most stamps are marked with something called a 'postmark', which means you can't use them again – but sometimes they aren't. When that happens, Mum claps her hands like it's Christmas morning, carefully peels the stamp away so that it looks just as brand new as possible, and puts it in her stamp box.

I picked out three that had the nicest pictures with the colour purple in them and a '1st' in the corner. I knew that most letters just had one stamp on them, but I thought three might make the letter get to the Queen faster. Especially since there was a chance I might miss the five o'clock post – trying to keep things a secret when there's a grown-up around always makes everything take twice as long.

I told Mrs Abbey I was doing my homework early and coloured in lots of purple swirls on the front of the envelope and then, just before I put the letter inside it, I thought the Queen should know about Ahmet's sister and the sea. So I wrote:

P.S. Ahmet had a little sister called Syrah but she died in the sea. So he needs to find his Mum and Dad even more spescially. Please keep this a Secret.

I knew what had happened to Ahmet's sister was a secret, but last year Mr Thompson told us that the Queen has to keep State Secrets. And if she can keep secrets about the state of everything, I knew she could keep Ahmet's secrets safe for him too.

THE EMERGENCY PLAN

After I had posted the letter, I felt as if a thousand worms and butterflies and frogs had all jumped into my tummy, and were wriggling and squirming and hopping around together. I was even too excited to finish my chocolate chip cookies and glass of milk which are my favourite Friday treats!

When Mum got home, she kept looking at me and putting her hand on my head to see if I was feeling ill. I wanted more than anything to tell her about the Greatest Idea in the World, but we had all agreed to keep it secret and I thought it would be more fun to surprise Mum with it all later. I spent the whole weekend trying to stay as quiet as I could in case my mouth said something when I wasn't paying attention. And even when Mum took me to a farm to see goats and donkeys and rabbits for our Sunday Adventure, I couldn't help thinking about the Queen, and if she'd gotten our letter yet. The whole weekend seemed to take for ever to finish, but just when I thought it never would, Monday morning finally arrived.

When I got to the bus stop, Tom and Josie and Michael were all waiting.

'She must have read it by now!' said Michael, bumping into a lamp post in his excitement.

We all paused as he quickly regained his balance and put his glasses straight.

'And I bet her Special Policemen are looking for Ahmet's family already,' said Josie, starting to half-skip and half-walk again, bouncing her football up and down with a loud twang.

'Yeah, I bet they're jumping from special planes right now to find all of them!' said Tom, gripping the straps of his rucksack as if it was really a parachute.

We were still chatting excitedly as we got onto the bus and spent the whole journey imagining what else the Queen might be doing to help Ahmet.

But Monday passed by, and even though I looked up at Mrs Khan after every break-time, hoping she had something special to say, there was no sign that anything had happened at all. Ms Hemsi looked normal too, and when we asked Ahmet if anything exciting had happened to him, he looked puzzled and then said, 'Bag not smell any more. Look!' before opening his rucksack and inviting each of us to smell it.

On Tuesday, it was the same; except this time, all of us were feeling more worried than excited, and the worms and butterflies and frogs in my tummy were starting to make me feel sick.

'What if she never got the letter?' whispered Josie, as we were all making a drawing of different planets in the solar system. 'What if it got lost in the post?'

'I don't know,' I whispered back, because I really didn't.

'We have to think of something else!' said Tom, glancing around to make sure Mrs Khan wasn't looking. 'We've only got three days left until the gates close!'

'Tom! Back to work please,' ordered Mrs Khan, looking our way.

We all quickly put our heads down low.

I snuck a look over my shoulder at Ahmet, who was busy colouring in a large orange circle that was obviously Mars. Tom was right. For whatever reason, the Queen wasn't helping us. We needed to think of something else. We needed an Emergency Plan.

I looked at my half-finished drawing of the planet Earth, and turning it over, decided to draw out an Emergency Plan instead.

While everyone else copied out facts about their planets to learn off by heart, I stared at the Emergency Plan and wondered if it would work. I wasn't sure that it would, but Dad always said that you could only ever know if something would work or not after you had tried it out first.

That afternoon, on the bus home, I showed the others my Emergency Plan.

Josie looked at me and, placing her football underneath her chin, shook her head. 'That's crazy.'

'Yeah. We can't do that! We'd get detentions for a year!' said Tom.

'It's the ONLY way,' I said, looking at it carefully.

This is what it looked like:

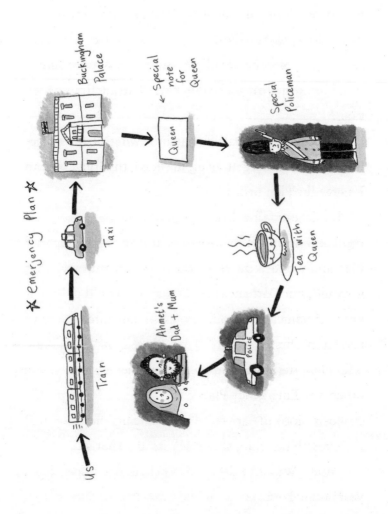

183

Michael shook his head. 'We'll get . . . *expelled*,' he whispered, looking around the bus to make sure no one had overheard anything.

'No, we won't,' I said, trying to sound more sure.

'The Special Police would never let us in to see her,' said Michael.

'They will when we explain everything,' I said. 'We'll go when she's having her tea – that way we can be sure she's in.'

Everyone fell silent. I could tell they were all thinking extra hard, because Josie was biting her bottom lip and Tom was looking down at his tie with a frown and Michael was tapping a finger on the lens of his glasses.

After a few seconds, Tom looked up and asked, 'How will we afford the Tube ticket?'

'It's OK,' I said, leaning in. 'I've got some pocket money saved up.'

'How much have you got?' asked Josie.

'Four pounds and fifty-five pence,' I whispered, so that nobody on the bus would hear. It would have been more, but I had bought some extra sweets last week.

'That's not enough for a ticket,' tutted Michael.

'I've got eleven pounds and thirty-two pence at home we can use.'

'I'll bring all my pocket money too,' said Josie.

'Me too,' said Tom. 'And all my brothers'!'

'But how are we going to *get* the Tube tickets?' asked Michael. 'Won't the ticket office people tell the police on us if they see us without a grown-up?'

'We won't go to the ticket office – we'll just get them from the ticket machines,' I said. 'I know how to use them. Mum shows me how to buy tickets all the time when we go on our Adventures.'

'Cool!' said Josie, looking more sure.

'So ... shall we all do it then? Tomorrow?' I whispered.

Josie nodded and twirled the football around between her fingers.

Michael looked around and, pushing up his glasses, gave a nod too.

And Tom looked over at Josie and Michael before giving me a thumbs-up.

'OK,' I said, as I tapped the end of my pencil against my cheek and looked at the plan again. 'I'll get some teabags – just in case she's not expecting us and runs out ...'

'I'll get some biscuits . . .' promised Tom.

'I'll bring as much pocket money as I can,' said Michael.

'And maybe we can all get a gift for the Queen,' added Josie. 'You know – to make her want to help us.'

'Should we wear anything special?' asked Tom. 'Don't people get dressed up when they're meeting the Queen – like hats and dresses and crowns and things? Maybe we should put on our best clothes underneath our uniforms.'

'Yeah, that's a brilliant idea!' I said. 'And we can get changed in the toilets at the palace.'

'Hold on . . .' Michael looked at us, his large eyes even rounder and wider. 'We can't ALL go, can we? Mrs Khan won't believe us if we say we're all sick on the exact same day – and what if she calls our parents?'

Everyone fell quiet again. We all wanted to go and see the Queen together, but Michael was right.

After a few seconds, Josie said, 'I can stay behind. My parents don't like me being friends with Ahmet anyway – they'd probably get really mad if they find out I ran away from school for him.'

'Let me go!' said Tom. 'My uncle's a policeman in New York and says 4-1-1 and Tango, Fox, Chicken and things, so I can talk to the Queen's Special Police.'

Michael sighed. 'OK. So I'll stay too. Even though I've always wanted to meet the Queen . . .'

'OK then. Tom will come with me,' I said.

'Quick – it's our stop!' cried out Josie, frantically pushing the bell.

Later that night, as I got ready for bed, I wondered what Dad would have said if he knew I was going on an adventure to try and meet the Queen. I think he would have put on a record and danced around the living room just like he did whenever he was really happy.

That last thought made all the worms and frogs and butterflies in my tummy settle down, and helped me fall into a deep sleep, filled with dreams of my dad dancing with the Queen.

STAN THE TAXI MAN

I'm not sure if Tintin ever woke up on the morning of an adventure feeling hungry and sick at the *exact* same time. But that's how I felt when I woke up the next day.

It was so early that the birds had only just started to sing, and the sun hadn't risen properly yet. As soon as the sky began to turn from dark blue to golden-pink, I jumped out of bed and started to get ready. The hardest thing was trying to fit my school uniform over my best clothes – it made me look all puffy like a blowfish, and the buttons on my school shirt looked like they might pop open at any moment. But luckily Mum didn't notice anything because she was tired and was still rubbing her eyes a lot when I left.

I got to the bus stop fifteen minutes early just like we said we would, but there was no one there except an old lady, and two grown-ups in suits.

After a few minutes, Tom came running up the road. I could tell right away that he hadn't slept much because his eyes looked red and his usually spiky hair was flat in the back.

Then came Josie, looking as excited and nervous as I felt inside, and Michael, who tripped over his shoelaces and stumbled but kept on running up to us anyway.

'Got everything?' asked Josie.

I nodded, and showed her the tube map I had taken from my Mum's Used-Less Drawer and the tea bags I had taken from the kitchen jar.

We'd all brought things to give to the Queen. Tom had brought a packet of shortbread biscuits, Josie had a new packet of football stickers, and Michael had brought a box of fudge that had a crown on the box. I had brought my favourite astronaut ruler. Even though the astronaut didn't move any more, I was sure the Queen would like it because she always wears sparkling brooches that shine like stars on her dresses. Maybe when she was in school, she wanted to be an astronaut too.

When we had stored all the presents away safely in my bag, Josie counted all the money we had collected. All of us had emptied out our piggy banks and savings jars and Tom had gone into his brothers' rooms to see what he could find.

'They've got loads of coins everywhere! Can't believe I've never done it before!' he exclaimed, bringing out a fistful of coins.

In the end, we had exactly twenty-seven pounds and sixty-two pence. A fortune!

'Half of twenty-seven pounds and sixty-two pence is . . .' Josie squeezed her eyes tight and quickly did the maths in her head. 'Thirteen pounds and eighty-one pence!' She gave half of the money to me and half to Tom for safe-keeping.

'You sure you know which Tube to take?' asked Josie. The freckles on her face were sliding up and down because she was scrunching up her nose every few seconds. She only ever does that when she's extra nervous and it makes her look like a hamster.

'Yup. We take the pink line to King's Cross, and

then the dark blue line to Green Park,' I said. 'Mum always takes me on the trains for our Really Big Adventures so I know the way.'

'How far is the palace from the train station?' asked Tom. His voice sounded squeaky but I couldn't tell if that was because he was nervous or excited.

'I don't know,' I said. 'But I don't think there's a bus stop in front of the palace so we might need to take a taxi. It shouldn't be too far though, so hopefully we won't spend all our money.'

'Guys, our bus is here!' said Michael, as he stuck out his hand so that the bus driver would stop.

'Remember what to tell Mrs Khan!' I whispered loudly. 'That me and Tom are sick and that our mums said we'll be back tomorrow!'

Josie nodded. 'Good luck!' And giving us a quick wave, she followed Michael onto the bus to school.

After the bus had disappeared, Tom and I crossed the street and walked up to the bus stop where all the buses travelling in the opposite direction stopped.

When the bus we needed finally came, I put out my hand and we got on, nervously looking at the bus driver in case she asked us why we weren't in school. But she didn't; in fact, she barely even looked at us.

We sat on the bus all the way to the last stop, and then, holding hands, crossed the big road to the Tube station.

There were at least a million people all dressed in suits, rushing around trying to get through the barriers. They looked angry and red in the face, and there was lots of tutting and head-shaking. I had never been to the train station when it was so busy before, and I didn't like it. It made my head feel hot and fuzzy.

'Come on,' said Tom, nudging me.

We walked over to the ticket machines where there was a long line of people. Some of them looked down at us with frowns on their faces, but no one said anything, so we didn't have to say anything back.

When we finally got to the front of the queue, we walked up to one of the machines. It looked more scary than I remembered. There were at least a hundred buttons surrounding a large screen, and a slot that looked like a letterbox at the bottom.

'Go on,' whispered Tom.

'OK,' I said, not wanting to be a coward. I took a deep breath, stood up on my toes, and walked over to the screen. I pressed the button for 'New Ticket', then 'Child' and then typed in 'Buk-Kingham Palace' for the destination, but nothing happened.

I tried again, but the machine started flashing.

'Do you kids need help?' asked a woman from the queue. She was dressed in a green coat and shiny shoes and had curly black hair and glasses.

Tom's eyes became wide and he shook his head, but I nodded.

The woman stepped forward. 'Where do you need to go?' she asked.

'Buk-Kingham Palace,' I said. 'For – our school trip.' I tried to make my voice more deep and grown-up sounding.

The woman frowned but then, looking at her watch, said, 'OK.' She quickly pressed lots of buttons on the screen, then said, 'There you go,' before stepping back into the line again.

We looked up at the machine which was flashing '£8.90' at us. Tom quickly got the money out of his bag and put in the exact change. Two pieces of pink card instantly popped out like sweets from a sweet machine, and, grabbing them, we thanked the lady and ran down the stairs to where I knew the trains for the city would be.

We squeezed ourselves onto the platform. It was so full of people that I was afraid we wouldn't be able to get on the train – I had never seen so many people squashed together in one place before.

But when the train came, everyone flooded onto it like a giant wave and took us with them. Tom grabbed hold of my arm and I grabbed his and we soon found ourselves pressed like sandwich filling between lots of people, all busy looking at their phones or listening to music.

'This . . . is . . . good . . .' said Tom, his face squashed up against a large belly. I tried to nod but someone's book was touching my head.

We watched as lots of stations passed by and looked at all the different people getting on and off the train. Finally, we heard the driver announce that the next station was going to be King's Cross.

'We have to follow the dark blue line,' I said to Tom after we had jumped out onto the platform. We followed signs for the Piccadilly Line and got on another train. Easy!

Now that I wasn't feeling so nervous, I realised I was hungry. I had been so busy packing a present for the Queen, I had forgotten about the emergency bag of sweets I had meant to bring.

'Do you think the Queen would mind if we had one of her biscuits?' I asked Tom.

He shook his head eagerly. 'She must have lots in her kitchen. Especially if she has tea every day!'

He ripped open the packet and passed me one of the thick crumbly fingers that lay inside. It was the most delicious biscuit I had ever had – probably because I knew it was meant to be eaten by the Queen.

We had another biscuit each on the train, and after just a few minutes, the train lady announced, 'The next station is Green Park. Please alight here for the Jubilee and Victoria Lines'.

I like the train lady. She has a nice voice. I imagine she looks like Mary Poppins and sits at the very front of the train next to the driver in her own special chair. It must be fun going through all the stations and telling people which ones are coming next.

We hurried off the train and followed the signs to the taxis.

Running up the stairs, we found a long line of black cabs waiting in a row. Inside the one at the front was a man with curly red hair. He was eating a sandwich and bobbing his head along to the radio station.

When he saw us looking at him through the window, he rolled it down and leaned out.

'What can I do for you two?'

'Please, we need to get to Buk-King-Ham Pa-lace,' I said, just as loudly and clearly as I could – because I remembered my Uncle Lenny saying that there was nothing taxi drivers hated more than people who didn't say where they wanted to go clearly enough.

The Taxi Man leaned forward and looked around.

'Why are you on your own?' he asked, frowning.

'Er. We're meeting our teacher there. We're on a trip and we got separated from our class and our teacher said that if anyone got lost we had to meet the class there,' said Tom, all in a rush.

The Taxi Man frowned again and rubbed his chin.

'All right,' he said eventually. 'Hop in! And be quick about it! I ain't here to be chauffeuring lost kids around all day! You're lucky it's only a few minutes away and I've got tykes of me own!'

196

We jumped in quickly. The Taxi Man locked the doors and, in a single move, swerved off. As he drove out onto the main road, he looked at us in the funny rectangular shaped mirror that cars always have right at the front. Uncle Lenny says they're there so that drivers can check the traffic behind them. But I think they're there so that drivers can look at people sitting in the back seat when they think no one is looking at them.

'What will you be doing at Buckingham Palace today then?' he asked.

'We're going to meet the Queen,' said Tom, before I could stop him.

'Is that right, now?' asked the Taxi Man, looking at us again in the mirror. His eyes were smiling.

Tom clapped his hands over his mouth and didn't say anything else. But the Taxi Man just laughed and said, 'Well, when you see her, say hi from me.'

I nodded, and the Taxi Man laughed again.

After a few minutes, the taxi came to a stop in traffic.

The Taxi Man looked at his watch. 'Ah – they'll be doing the changing of the guards soon. You'll have to walk from here I'm afraid.' He turned around to look at us and pointed to his right. 'See those arches there? Just walk under them and keep going straight down this big red road, OK? The palace is right at the end, past the water fountain.'

Tom nodded and took out the exact money it said on the meter.

The Taxi Man shook his head. 'Don't worry. This one's on me! Just tell your teacher to be more careful next time.'

'Thanks,' said Tom, as we jumped out. 'You're the best taxi driver ever!'

The Taxi Man drove off, laughing.

'I like London taxi drivers!' said Tom, taking out another two of the Queen's biscuits and stuffing them in his mouth. 'They're beh-er than eh New York ones!'

'So do I,' I said, watching as taxi disappeared out of sight.

THE QUEEN'S PALACE

'There are so many police,' whispered Tom, as we walked down the big, bright-red road. Everywhere we looked, there were lots of orange cones and police in yellow jackets sitting on horses.

'I know,' I whispered back. We didn't really need to whisper, but seeing so many police cars and officers was making us both nervous, especially as we weren't with a grown-up. 'Come on,' I said, pulling Tom behind me. 'Let's go!'

We walked just as fast as we could. But the red road was long and it felt as if we had been walking for miles before we finally saw the fountain the Taxi Man had told us about. 'Look!' said Tom, pointing up at the giant black gates of the palace. The spiked ends looked like they had been dipped in gold and there were hundreds of people everywhere. It looked like this:

'There must be something happening,' I said, looking around. 'I don't remember it being this busy when I came with Mum.'

The road ahead of us was filled with hundreds of people, lots of them with cameras around their necks. Some were talking and waving to the policemen, others were climbing the giant fountain and sitting on its short walls, and yet more were leaning against the grey barriers that had been placed all along the sides of the pavements. There were people with large cameras resting on their shoulders, looking like they were getting ready to film something, and huge helicopters that looked like giant dragonflies humming in the sky above and making the air shake.

'Maybe someone special's coming to visit?' suggested Tom.

'Let's go over there and find out,' I said, pointing to the two biggest gates that lay in front of the palace. Each gate had a golden crest that was almost as big as me stuck on them, and showed two lions dancing in front of some large spiky leaves. Two police officers, dressed all in black and with large stars in the middle of their helmets, were sitting on horses in front of both the gates, silently observing the crowds.

'Are those the Queen's police?' asked Tom, pointing to them. 'Shall we go and ask them if we can see her?'

I shook my head. 'The Queen's *Extra-Special* Police are the ones in the red jackets and giant hats. They're the Guards of the Palace – so we have to ask one of them. Come on. I'll show you!'

Holding each other's hands, we zigzagged our way through the crowd until we found a tiny gap in one of the grey barriers. Squeezing through it, we ran across the big red road until we reached the barriers next to where the big black and golden gates were. Trying to say, 'Excuse me!' and 'Sorry!' as we pushed our way past the crowds was hard work, but after a few minutes we finally reached the palace gates.

'See?' I said, pointing through the railings. '*Those* are the Special Guards! We need to get near to one of them.'

Tom pushed his face through two of the railings and stared at the Palace Guards. You can tell right away they're more special than the normal police because they wear bright red coats with extra shiny buttons, and they have coins on their chests and huge hairy hats that cover half their eyes. They also carry extra-pointy guns and stand as still as statues inside special tiny black houses.

The Palace Guards both suddenly said 'Hut!' and marched across the front of the palace like toy soldiers.

'Why do they say "Hut"?' asked Tom, watching with his mouth open.

'Because they're swapping huts,' I said, remembering what my mum had told me when I had asked her the same question.

'Oh. Cool,' said Tom. 'So what do we do now? How do we give them our note for the Queen?'

'I don't know,' I said, realising that I must have remembered things wrong. When I had come with Mum, I was sure the guards had been standing much closer to the front gates. Now they were so far away we couldn't even send them the note by air mail – even if we could make it into a paper aeroplane that could fly straight!

I was wondering what we should do when, in the distance, a bell chimed eleven times.

When it had finished, a man in a bright blue tracksuit top standing next to us shouted, 'They're gonna start any minute now! Time to get your cameras ready!'

A large group of people standing in front of us quickly got out their cameras, and everywhere I looked, hundreds of people began doing the same thing.

Then, suddenly, everyone fell quiet. I looked back through the gates towards the palace. Both of the Palace Guards were standing extra still, and, like a sweet wrapper being crunched together every few seconds, we heard the distant sound of marching.

'LOOK!' cried out Tom, clinging onto the gates for a better view. He pointed towards the water fountain where, from far away, little dots of red and black and gold were marching and playing trumpets and drums.

'Let's get to the front,' I whispered, and, saying 'Sorry' and 'Excuse me please', we pushed our way back to the front near the grey barriers.

'Look – over there!' said Tom, prodding me as he pointed to where the two large palace gates stood closed. 'There's none of these barriers on the pavements there – see! We might be able to reach the guards better from there.' I leaned forwards just as far as I could and looked more closely.

Tom was right.

There were no barriers on that part of the pavement at all – which meant anyone standing there could easily pass a note to one of the guards as they marched into the palace!

'You're right – let's get closer,' I said.

But before we could push our way along the barriers to the corner of the pavement where there were none, we heard a police officer shout, 'Everyone, stand back! Stand back! The gates will now open!'

As the crowds surged forwards and forced us to press up against the barriers, we saw the large, gold-crested gates begin to swing open from the inside. The palace courtyard was now filled with lots of Palace Guards who had silently joined the two we had seen before, and were all standing still.

'Whoah – that's AWESOME!' cried Tom, his eyes wide and his cheeks pink as he pointed back up the main road towards the fountain. What had seemed like tiny flashes of red and gold and black from a distance had now transformed into hundreds of tall soldiers marching in time, as drums and trumpets filled the air. Led by a man dressed in a shimmering golden jacket who was carrying a stick topped by a diamond that was as big as a doorknob, they all marched towards the gates with a rush of energy that made the ground shudder.

I opened my mouth, but nothing came out. I had never, ever seen anything like this in real life before.

'Ten! Hut!' shouted someone from behind the palace gates. All the soldiers immediately stamped the ground with one foot and swivelled around on their extra shiny black boots to face the open gates.

'The man in the gold coat,' said Tom, poking me in the arm. 'He must be extra special – let's give *him* the note! But look . . . They're going in now!'

Everyone around us flashed their cameras as the man in the golden coat and the Palace Guards behind him marched closer and closer to the palace gates.

The other Guards waiting in the palace courtyard suddenly began to march on the spot, before beginning to march out through the gates.

'Oh! I GET IT!' exclaimed Tom. 'They're changing *over*! So *those* ones are going home, and *those* ones behind the man in the gold coat are going to stay here with the Queen!'

'But . . .' I turned around. 'That means the gates are going to be shut – as soon as the swap is done . . . and . . .' And when they were, we wouldn't have another chance to get our note to the Queen . . .

Tom looked at me with his mouth open, and I looked back at him with my mouth open, and I could tell we had both thought the exact same thought as each other.

Feeling my hands start to shake, I pulled the note out of my coat pocket and held it out. We had to do it – we had to! It wasn't every day that you got to go to the Queen's Palace and see her Special Guards so up close! But even though I tried to make my voice come out, it stayed stuck in my throat.

'Those – those are HUGE!' said Tom, looking at the guns the soldiers were holding over their shoulders. I was looking at them too. They were long and had extra-pointy ends that suddenly looked more sharp and shiny and much more pointier than they had done just a few minutes ago.

The man in the golden jacket and all the Palace Guards behind him were now beginning to march past us. In just a few seconds, they would be entering through the gates. And when they did and those gates were closed, there would be no chance of telling the Queen about Ahmet – and it would be all my fault.

I clutched the note tightly. I could feel my heart thumping in my throat, and my fingers beginning to sweat.

And then, somehow, I began to move.

I think when you're the most scared you've ever been in your life and have to do something you've never, ever done before, your brain switches off and your arms and legs do all the thinking for you which is why you feel as if you're moving underwater. That's what happened the moment I began running. I felt as though I was running underwater, and as if someone else was doing everything for me. When, of course, they weren't. It was all me.

I felt myself clambering over the barriers in front of me and slowly running out onto the red road. I could feel people's eyes turning to watch me and a sudden breeze on my face. From underneath my feet, I could feel the surprisingly bouncy surface of the road as if it was a soft red carpet, and in my hands I could feel the rough edges of the note. All around me, the sound of drums and trumpets and the crunching of boots faded away. And then suddenly I was there ... standing behind the last row of the Queen's Special Guards as they were walking into the palace. I watched as my right hand lifted itself higher and higher and higher, until it finally touched a red-coated elbow. And without me even telling it to, my mouth opened and shouted, 'EXCUSE ME, SIR!'

And that's when everything went funny.

Because suddenly the world sped back up, and there were people gasping and cameras flashing and hooves thundering, and helicopters helicoptering, and before I knew what was happening, a looming tower of policemen with extra shiny stars on their helmets surrounded me, blocking out the sky. Everything started to fade away into a sea of black, I felt my legs wobble like a big plate of runny jelly, and a crashing in my ears began to roar as the ground rushed up to meet me.

THE COLD STREAM GUARDS

When my brain woke up again and I opened my eyes, I was lying on something soft and could see a blur of flashing blue lights and lots of police cars everywhere.

'Right, let's get her in the ambulance,' said a voice.

Tom was standing next to where my feet were. He was crying and saying 'friend' a lot to a London police officer. But standing behind him were two of the Queen's Special Guards!

Forgetting that I had been frightened, I sat up and cried out, 'Please!' And, realising the note was still in my hand but all scrunched up now, I held it out to them and said, 'Please – you have to give this to the Queen . . .'

The London police officer who had been talking to Tom walked up to me. 'Now, you just calm down and take it easy. You did a dangerous thing today. These are trained combat officers,' he said, pointing at the Queen's Special Guards. 'They're trained to stop anyone attempting to hurt the Queen.'

'But – but we didn't want to hurt the Queen!' sobbed Tom, his face red and wet.

'We know that now, son, but we can't be too careful, can we?' said the officer, his voice not as strict as it was before.

One of the Queen's Special Guards came over to me. 'Let's have a look at this note then, shall we?' he said gently, holding out his hand.

I handed it to him and watched his face as he read it. Sometimes people won't tell you what they're really thinking, so you have to watch their face extra hard and see if they give any clues away. I didn't expect a Special Guard to do anything with his face – especially not one who worked for the Queen – but this one chuckled and then handed it over to the other Special Guard standing next to him and who had more medals on his chest. He smiled too. I don't know why, because it wasn't meant to be funny.

This is what the note said:

Dear your Highness Majesty Queen of England,

We wrote you a Letter on Friday about Ahmet, our friend who's a Refugee Boy and put three stamps on it so that the Royal Mail would get it to you faster. We've come to see you today because it's Wednesday already and we thought the Royal Mail might have lost the letter and as the gates are closing on Friday, it means we haven't got much time to find Ahmet's family and bring them here to so they can all live together.

We're outside the gates now. Tom's got brown hair and I've got dark brown hair and we're in our School uniforms which are dark blue and grey with pictures of a ship and a book on it so that you can see us easily.

We can't stay later then half past one because if we don't get home at home-time then our mums and Tom's dad and Josie and Michael will worry. Please let us come and see you as soon as you've finished your brekfast.

Yours Sinseerly, Me and Tom
P.S. We've got extra tea bags for tea.

'Hoping to have tea with the Queen there were you?' asked the second Special Guard as he shook his head. 'Here, take a look at this,' he said, passing the note to a police officer who was standing opposite. She read it and said, 'Well, you don't see notes like that every day.'

A Paramedic woman in a dark green onesie looked at the note too. 'Awww. Sweet,' she said. Then she made me lie down again, and started pushing the bed onto an ambulance.

'But I don't want to go to hospital! Please! No!' I shouted, starting to feel scared. I don't like hospitals. The last time I saw Dad was when he was in a hospital, and I made a promise to myself that I wouldn't ever see one again. Not ever.

'Don't worry. We won't take you to the hospital unless we need to, darling. But I do need to check you're OK and that you don't have a concussion,' said the Paramedic calmly. She had long black hair that was tied into a ponytail, and large brown eyes and an upside-down watch on her chest.

'Just lie here quietly for me for a few minutes, and we'll have you out and about in no time,' she added, giving me a wink. The wink and her nice voice made me feel a little better, so I did what she said.

After she pushed me onto the ambulance, the Paramedic told me her name was Davinder and asked me all sorts of things. Like how I was feeling and if I had a Head Ache and who Ahmet was and about my mum and dad. I told her about my dad and she said she was sorry. She held my wrist and checked my pulse and put a thermometer in my mouth, and then said, 'I just need to check your heartbeat.' But when she pulled up my school jumper, she stopped.

'Nice top,' she said, her mouth suddenly looking as if it was tickling her.

I looked down at myself and suddenly remembered that we had put on our best outfits for the Queen. 'It's my best top,' I said, touching the shirt dotted with sparkling silver stars and golden planets. 'For when we saw the Queen,' I explained.

'Ah!' grinned Paramedic Davinder, as she opened the top three buttons and put a cold silver disc on my chest. 'Now take a deep breath in . . . and out . . .'After listening for a moment, she nodded and said, 'You look and sound absolutely fine to me. Ready to go?' I nodded, so she helped me down from the bed and held my hand as I got off the ambulance. In the distance, I could hear people cheering, but I didn't know why.

'Now, I think it's time for you two to get on home. Officer Martina is going to take you both home in that special car over there,' said Paramedic Davinder. She pointed to the London police officer who was standing next to Tom and the two Special Guards. Behind her was a police car with flashing blue lights on top of it.

'*Really?*' asked Tom, his eyes lighting up.

I was excited too – but then I remembered the note.

'But – what about the Queen – and the note?' I cried, looking up at everyone. 'If we don't give it to the Queen then she won't know that we came and she won't know about Ahmet . . .'

Officer Martina smiled. 'Oh, I think she'll know you came all right!' she said.

The Special Guard wearing the most medals walked over to me and bent down so that his face was at the same level as mine. He had bright blue eyes and a large dimple in his cheek just like Dad used to have – only Dad had them in both cheeks, not just one.

'Her Majesty isn't here today,' he said. 'She's actually in her other castle in Windsor.'

'The Queen's got ANOTHER castle?' asked Tom, looking horrified.

'Don't worry. I'll make sure she knows you were both here and that she gets this.' The Special Guard held up the note. 'All right?'

'Promise?' I asked, suddenly feeling happy again. 'Like, really, *really* promise?'

'You have my word!' He nodded. 'And a Coldstream Guard never breaks their word.'

'What's a Cold Stream Guard?' I asked, immediately imagining lots of them diving into freezing cold streams with their hats on.

'A Coldstream Guard is what we are,' he replied, standing back up straight. 'I'm Lieutenant Chris Taylor, and standing next to your friend Tom there is Second Lieutenant Walter Kungu.' I looked over at the other guard, who was now giving us a salute. 'We're part of a very special force that protects both the Queen's houses and the country.'

'Can you give her our presents too, then?' asked Tom.

'Presents?' asked Officer Martina.

'Yeah – we got them for the Queen . . .' explained Tom, pulling out the half-eaten packet of biscuits, the ruler, the packet of football stickers and the squashed box of fudge from my rucksack.

'I'm afraid we can't take those,' grinned Lieutenant Kungu. 'But we'll let her know about them when we give Her Majesty your note.'

'Oh . . . OK . . .' Tom shrugged, stuffing everything back into my bag.

'Now, kids. Time to get you home,' said Officer Martina. 'We've spoken to your school and your parents and have told them what happened.'

'Oh noooo . . .' said Tom, twisting his hands. 'We're gonna be in so much trouble!'

I nodded miserably.

'Don't worry,' said Paramedic Davinder. 'I'm sure they'll be happy just to have you back home and safe. And I *think* . . .' she added, looking up at the helicopters that were flying overhead. 'You might even be a little bit famous!'

Tom frowned at me and I frowned back, because we were both wondering what could have made us famous.

'You two have a safe journey now,' said Lieutenant Taylor.

'And the next time you want to send the Queen a message, don't go running after any of us soldiers,' said Lieutenant Kungu. 'A letter is more than enough!'

And, giving Tom and me a nod and a salute, the Queen's Special Cold Stream Guards who were now Extra-Extra Special to both Tom and me, marched off back towards the palace, carrying the Queen's note.

'Right, young troopers! In you go,' said Officer Martina, as a silver car with bright yellow and blue squares on its doors and a huge siren on the top stopped in front of us.

Passing me a piece of folded paper, Paramedic Davinder said, 'That's a special note for your mum – to let her know you're completely fine. So make sure you give it to her, OK?'

I nodded.

'Bye then,' smiled Paramedic Davinder, as she began to wave. 'You both take care of yourselves now . . .'

Getting into the back seat of the police car, we waved back. Lots of people also began cheering and waving at us from all along the palace walls, so we waved back at them too, even though we didn't really know why.

Tom got out a biscuit and started eating it. I took one too, but even though I was hungry I couldn't eat it. My stomach felt all jumpy and twisty inside. And the closer we got to home, the more jumpy and twisty it became.

There are some journeys you can't ever enjoy no matter how exciting they are – not even when you're in a real police car. Because at the end of it, you know you'll be getting at least a hundred detentions and probably won't be allowed any pocket money or chocolate for ten years.

But it was OK. Because even not being able to have any chocolate ever again would be worth it if the Queen could help Ahmet find his mum and dad. That was all that really mattered.

21

THE NEIGHBOURS AND THE NEWS

Sometimes grown-ups can be so confusing that they make you scratch your head.

When Officer Martina took me home, Mum was the angriest I had ever seen her before. At first it was scary, because she kept shouting things like, 'I can't BELIEVE you did this!' and 'WHAT IF SOMETHING HAD HAPPENED TO YOU!' But then she would hug me and hold me so tight that I thought my bones were going to be crushed. I wasn't quite sure if I was being told off or not.

When she had calmed down, Mum made me hot soup and told me to tell her everything. So, I told her about Ahmet's pictures and about what the man and woman on the bus had said about the gates, and the

Greatest Idea in the World and the Emergency Plan and everything that had happened in front of the Queen's Palace. Mum was quiet while I talked and then, after I had finished telling her everything, she sat still for a long time and didn't say anything at all. I was too scared to say anything else, so I sat on my hands and stared at the table.

Finally, Mum opened her mouth to say something – but then the doorbell rang.

'Who's that I wonder?' Mum said. When she opened the door, Mrs Gillingham, the neighbour who lived next door to Mrs Abbey, was standing outside.

She always wears lots of necklaces and bright pink nail varnish and long dangly earrings. I like her because she smells like puff pastry and, at Christmas, she always gives me a stocking filled with sweets.

'Oh, hiya, love!' cried out Mrs Gillingham. She gave me a hug. 'Thank goodness you're back safe and sound! But my, that was brave of you, wasn't it? The woman on the news said it was so you could help the refugees!'

'Sorry, Mrs Gillingham?' said Mum, frowning. 'Did you just say you heard about it on the *news*?'

'Ooooh! It's all over the telly! ALL over it!' said Mrs Gillingham, excitedly. 'I expect you'll hear from the reporters soon!'

'Well ... yes ... Thank you for letting us know, Mrs Gillingham.' Mum started to close the door. 'We'd better get some rest. It's been a long day ...'

She waved Mrs Gillingham out of the door and then looked down at me. 'Hm. The news ...'

Just then the doorbell rang again.

'Who is it?' called out Mum.

'It's Mr Rashid,' came a man's voice. There was a loud 'Ouch!' before he added, 'And Mrs Rashid!'

Mum looked at me in surprise and opened the door again.

This time, exactly where Mrs Gillingham had been standing, were Mr and Mrs Rashid. They lived one floor below us and have twins. You can tell when they're home because they always leave the pushchair in the landing – it's too big to fit through their front door.

We usually only ever see them in the lift or when they need help getting the pushchair out of the main door, but I liked them. Especially Mrs Rashid, because she wears the brightest clothes. Once she wore a long flowing dress that had millions of tiny sequins on it and made her shine like a goldfish. She's always smiling and laughing with the babies, and Mr Rashid likes to shout out the cricket scores to anyone he can find. But this was the first time they had ever come to our flat.

'Hello,' said Mum.

Mrs Rashid held up her phone. 'We've just read all about it!' she cried, shoving it into Mum's hand and pointing to a news story with a picture of lots of Palace Guards standing around someone lying on the floor. 'You were so brave. Now the Queen herself can't ignore what's happening to those families! I haven't slept for months, thinking about it. Months! It makes me so angry. All those poor people with their little babies, trying to just . . . *live* . . .'

'We send baby clothes and shoes whenever we can, but we don't have much money to spare,' continued Mr Rashid, his voice suddenly heavy and wobbly.

'And now . . .' Mrs Rashid spotted me over Mum's shoulder and bent down. 'Oh, you darling! Please, let me hug you!'

I hesitated for a moment – I don't always like being hugged. But Mrs Rashid seemed nice, so I slowly walked over to her and let her hug me and then hugged her back.

'If your refugee friend needs any help, *any* at all, please tell us,' she said, touching my cheeks. 'Yes?'

'Promise?' said Mr Rashid, his eyes big and serious.

I nodded, because I knew Ahmet would probably like Mr and Mrs Rashid and wouldn't mind me asking them for help for him.

'Good. Now you take care,' grinned Mr Rashid, as he and Mrs Rashid turned away and headed down the stairs.

'Well. This is turning out into quite a day, isn't it?' laughed my mum, looking down at me and giving my shoulders a squeeze.

But before she could close the door, Mr Greggs' huge head suddenly popped in.

I took a step back and hid behind my mum because I don't like Mr Greggs at all, even though he always dresses in a suit and takes his hat off whenever he sees anyone he likes.

I can tell Mum doesn't like him either because she never says 'Hello' to him when we see him, and my mum always says hello to everyone. Even the man who sleeps in the doorway of Mr Polezki's shop on the corner of our road.

'Yes, Mr Greggs. What can I do for you?' asked Mum in her most polite voice. She only ever uses that voice when she talks to people she doesn't like. Like Aunt Christina or the man with the clipboard who calls himself Land Lord.

Mr Greggs cleared his throat and said, 'I've just dropped by to say that your daughter there would do well to mind her own business. Those pesky refugees are only here because they want a piece of our benefits pie! She ought to know better – and *you* ought to have taught her better.'

I looked up at Mum's face and saw that it had gone as white as one of our dinner plates, as she stared at Mr Greggs without blinking.

'Have you finished?' she said, in a voice that was so cold I didn't recognise it.

'All I'm saying is that your child was nearly *killed* today for immigrant pests that want the easy life without having to work a day for it! I mean, I know you're not exactly white but you've been here long enough to know better – surely?'

'Mr Greggs! That is QUITE enough!' said Mum, her voice cold and formal. Her eyes had narrowed, and her hands had become tight little balls. 'You and your views are not welcome here. Please leave.'

And taking a step back, Mum slammed the door shut just as loudly as she could so that one second Mr Greggs was there, and the next second, he wasn't. We could hear him ranting at us from the other side, but, after a few seconds, his voice started to get fainter and fainter.

'*Despicable* man!' muttered Mum, clicking the extra bolt on the door shut. 'With his dinner jackets and silly neckerchiefs trying to cover up his bigotry . . .'

'Why is he so angry, Mum?' I asked, slipping my hand into hers. 'And why did he call refugees "pests"?'

'Because he's a heartless, selfish man, who hates everyone far too much to want to help anyone,' said Mum. 'Even refugee children like Ahmet.'

'Oh,' I said, wondering how anyone could hate someone who was running away from bullies and bombs. Mr Greggs had clearly never met someone like Ahmet before, because if he had, he could never have been so horrible about anyone who had to become a refugee.

'Now, let's forget about Mr Greggs and go see what the news is saying about you, shall we?' She ruffled my hair and then went and switched on the telly as I did a running jump onto the sofa.

After a few seconds, a newsreader flashed up onto the screen. Her voice was warm as she said, 'Today, an incident at Buckingham Palace added an extra few steps to the Changing of the Guard ceremony, as a nine-year-old child ran out and intercepted one of the Queen's Coldstream Guards.'

As she talked the picture changed and I appeared on the screen, running out of the crowd and reaching up to touch a Palace Guard's arm with Tom just a few steps behind me. I looked so scared that it made me wonder how I had done what I did. I had never, ever seen anyone I knew on the television before, and it was the strangest thing in the world to not only see myself on it, but to have done something that a newsreader was talking about.

'It transpired that the child in question wanted to hand in a note for the Queen, appealing for help on behalf of a refugee boy searching for his parents following their joint escape from the ongoing conflict in Syria. We are expecting an official response from Buckingham Palace later this evening.'

Mum quickly flicked over to the next channel. Another newsreader was talking, and behind him was another picture of me, looking shocked and scared.

'The Queen's Guard had an unexpected encounter today, as a young child broke through the barriers during the famed Changing of the Guard ceremony. It is said the attack was made in protest against the government's poor handling of the refugee crisis.'

'But I didn't attack anyone!' I cried out. Mum nodded but didn't say anything, and instead switched the channel to another newsreader.

This third newsreader confused me the most, because he said: 'A nine-year-old child sparked a terrorist alert today after disturbing the Changing of the Guard ceremony, and raising wider questions around security . . .'

Mum leaned over and turned off the sound.

'But I didn't want to hurt anyone!' I said, trying not to cry. 'Why do they think I'm a ter-terror-ist?'

Mum sighed sadly and, opening up her arms, pulled me towards her. 'There are lots of silly people in the world darling, people who are so afraid of anyone who doesn't look like them or dress like them or eat the same food as them that they call other people – even children like you – all sorts of silly names.'

'But I eat everything!' I said, confused. 'Except broccoli and baked beans. And what's wrong with what I wear?'

'Nothing at all,' said Mum. 'But they might still be scared of you because you don't look like them,' she said, stroking my hand.

'So . . . I'm *scary*? Just because I look different?' I asked.

Mum nodded. 'Yes. Silly isn't it?'

I leaned back against my mum and fell into a Deep Thought. That's when your brain falls down into a giant hole in the middle of your mind and has to try and put all the pieces of a Thought together so that it makes sense. And because your brain is working so hard, you can't think or talk about or see anything else. All you can really do is think about the Deep Thought.

The Deep Thought my brain had found was wondering how anyone could be scared of me just because I didn't look like them. Everyone in school looks different and likes different things – and has parents who come from all kinds of different places. Tom's mum and dad come from different places in America – one called Florida and the other called California. Michael's mum comes from a place called Nigeria, and his dad comes from France, which is why he always goes on lots of holidays and has even seen a giraffe and an elephant in the forest. Josie's mum comes from Barking and her dad comes from Bradford, which is why they speak differently, and her dad always sounds like he's asking a question, even when he isn't. And Mum and Uncle Lenny were both born in a faraway place I've never been to called Indonesia and my dad was born in Austria. Mrs Abbey once said that I was lucky to have parents from different places, because it meant I never needed to go on holiday to get a suntan.

I like looking like I have a suntan, and I like everyone being different. It would be too boring if everyone was exactly the same as each other.

'Mum?' I asked, because the Deep Thought was starting to give me a Head Ache. 'Does that mean the Queen's Special Guards were scared of me too?'

Mum looked at me and asked, 'Did they *seem* scared of you?'

'No,' I said, after thinking hard. 'They were nice.'

'Well then,' she replied, stroking my hair. 'The thing you have to remember, is that for every silly person who's afraid of you, there are at least twenty people who aren't silly at all.'

'OK,' I said, feeling better. It was good to know that there were more nice people in the world than there were silly people in it.

Just then, a face I knew popped up onto the television screen.

'Mum! Look! It's the Taxi Man!' I shouted, excitedly. 'He took us from the station to the Queen's Palace – and he wouldn't take our money!'

Mum put the sound up and we both listened, as a big red sign with 'Stan O'Connell, Taxi Driver' popped up underneath the picture of his smiling face.

'They were just kids,' he was saying cheerfully. 'Innocent kids, you know?'

A man next to him, who must have been the reporter because he was holding a microphone, said, 'And you didn't get the impression they were planning any sort of protest or attack?'

Mum made an angry sound in her throat and I saw her shake her head.

But Stan the Taxi Man smiled again and said, 'I didn't get that impression because that wasn't what happened. You can ask me another five times though – if you like!'

That made Mum burst out laughing, and she said she was glad I had met a cabbie who was as good and as funny as my Uncle Lenny was.

Just then the phone started to ring. It was my Uncle Lenny checking to make sure I was OK. And after he rang, lots of other people rang too, but they weren't people we knew – they were reporters from newspapers. In the end, Mum turned the phone off and said it was time to put this adventure to bed – because tomorrow would bring with it a brand new adventure to go on.

Mum let me go to bed a whole thirty minutes late that night, because I wanted to watch the news again. Lots of people had taken pictures and videos of me running onto the road. It was strange seeing things that I hadn't been able to see for myself at the time, even though I had been there and it had all happened to me. I hadn't realised how exciting it had been. As soon as I had run out onto the road, the police had started shouting and moving the crowd back and surrounded me in a big circle, and all the Special Guards had stopped playing their drums and trumpets and slammed the palace doors shut. It felt as if I was watching a movie starring someone that looked like me, but wasn't me at all.

I lay in bed that night trying to make sense of everything that had happened. But my brain felt fuzzy and tired, so in the end I gave up and closed my eyes. None of it really mattered, anyway. What mattered was that we had given our note to the Special Guards, and they had given us their word that they would tell the Queen about Ahmet.

And just as soon as they did, she would send out her Special Guards to find Ahmet's family. Before the gates closed shut, and it was too late.

WORLD WIDE WHISPERS

Instead of going to work the next morning, Mum decided to walk to the bus stop with me. She said it was because me and Tom were famous now, and that even though we probably wouldn't be famous for more than a day, we needed to be careful.

'I just want to make sure you're not going to be chased by any reporters,' she said, as she helped me put my coat on. 'Some of them are good people doing their job, but *some* of them have absolutely no scruples!'

I followed Mum out of the flat, wondering what 'scruples' were, because Mum had looked angry when she had said the word, so I knew it was bad not to have any of them. I also wondered why reporters might chase us. Tintin, who has to be one of the best reporters in the world, only ever chased people who were kidnappers or thieves or had done something wrong.

When we reached the bus stop, we found Tom's mum and dad there too. Mum went to talk to them and Tom and I huddled together.

Tom said his parents had told him that if he ever ran away from school again, he would be so grounded that he would never see daylight again.

'But I told Mum it comes in through the curtains anyway – even when they're shut. And then when we watched the news, she screamed and hugged me and said how brave I was,' said Tom, scratching his head. 'I don't get it.'

I told him I didn't get it either, and about everything that had happened to me after I had gotten home too – all the neighbours coming over, and about horrible Mr Greggs and how Mum had been angry one moment and then happy the next moment, and how she had laughed at what Stan the Taxi Man had said.

'Oh yeah – Dad gave him a cheer too,' Tom grinned. 'I've never seen him cheer for anything before. Except when we dropped off my nana at the airport after she'd been staying with us for a month . . .'

We heard footsteps, and Josie and Michael came running up to meet us.

'We saw you on the news!'

'Did you give them the note? What did they say?'

As soon as Josie and Michael finished asking their questions, Tom and me took it in turns to answer them. As we were talking, lots of people gathered round and asked me and Tom if we were the kids from the news. We were about to say yes, when Tom's dad called us over.

'Now listen up,' said Tom's dad, kneeling down. 'There are going to be a *lot* of people wanting to ask you all sorts of things about yesterday. And whilst you can tell Josie and Michael and Mrs Sanders everything—'

'And Mrs Khan?' I added.

'Yes – and Mrs Khan . . .'

'And Ms Hemsi?' asked Josie.

'OK, yes. Her too,' nodded Tom's dad, scratching his head in the exact same way Tom does when he's thinking. 'But if anyone *else* asks you what happened, I want you to say *exactly* what grown-ups say when they're famous and they've got to keep something a secret. Shall I tell you what that is?'

We all nodded and looked at each other excitedly.

'Famous grown-ups always say, "No comment" when they want to keep something a secret,' continued Tom's father. 'And that's what I want you to do. Let's all give it a practice right now. Tom, you go first.'

'No comment!' said Tom, thrusting his nose in the air.

'No comment!' said Josie, grinning.

'No comment!' said Michael, seriously.

'No comment!' I said, loudly.

'Good,' said Mum. 'Now, if anyone asks why you went to Buckingham Palace, or what the police said to you, or anything about yesterday, you say . . .?'

'NO COMMENT!' we all shouted, making all the people at the bus stop look over at us.

My mum and Tom's mum and dad all smiled.

'Now, there's a promise we want you all to make too,' said Mum. 'We want you all to promise us that you *won't* look at any newspapers today.'

We all looked at each other, frowning a little, but nodded.

'Promise?' asked Tom's mum. 'Not a single newspaper?'

'We promise,' we all said, although I could see Josie had her fingers crossed behind her back.

'Excellent,' said Tom's dad, giving us all a thumbs-up.

'Now, we've spoken to Mrs Sanders this morning,' said Tom's mum. 'And a teacher – probably Mrs Sanders herself – will be meeting you at the gates to make sure you don't get hounded by the odd reporter or two. You'll be taken straight to her office because she needs to have a few words with all of you before lessons start.'

'Oh no,' cried out Michael. 'Are we all in trouble – are my parents going to find out?'

'It'll be fine, son,' said Tom's dad, patting Michael on the back. 'I promise.'

'Now go on – have a good day,' said Mum, as our bus came to a loud, hissing stop in front of us. 'And we'll see you tonight – you're all to come straight home!' she shouted.

We all nodded and waved, and ran up to the top deck as usual. The other passengers looked at me and Tom with a frown before looking at their newspapers and then looking back at us again. We hurried past and sat together in a little huddle.

In whispers, Josie and Michael told us about their day yesterday. It had been exciting too. Josie said she'd had to make up a story involving a Chinese takeaway and endless buckets of puke to get Mrs Khan to believe I was sick but would be back the next day, and Michael had pretended to lose his voice so that he didn't have to say anything to Mrs Khan when she asked him where Tom was. But of course, he had kept forgetting that he was meant to have lost his voice, so Josie had to kick him lots of times to make him remember. And then, when the police had rung to tell Mrs Sanders what had happened, she had come and taken them both out of class, and made them tell her everything.

'Er . . . did Mrs Sanders say anything about giving us detention?' asked Tom.

Josie and Michael shook their heads.

'But Mrs Khan seemed upset,' said Josie, looking down. 'I feel bad for lying to her.'

'Me too,' said Michael.

'Maybe we should make her a card,' said Josie.

'Yeah. And I've still got some of the Queen's biscuits left over – we can give her those for her tea,' said Tom.

But when we got to school, we forgot all about Mrs Khan, because the school was surrounded by hundreds of vans with large round satellite dishes on their roofs, and lights and microphones and fluffy grey things on sticks. Staring at us were hundreds of cameras on legs, which looked like one-eyed insects that could zoom their eyes in and out and swivel their heads in any direction they wanted. And all of them had lots of people bobbing up and down behind them.

As we walked towards the gates, a woman suddenly cried out, 'There they are!' and started running towards us. I could see Mr Irons standing by the railings and looking at us, his eyes narrowed and his nose high in the air. His moustache was twitching.

'No comment!' shouted Michael, as he began running towards the school gates. We all ran too but before we could reach them, lots of cameras and arms and legs had surrounded us and were blocking our way.

'What message were you trying to send our government?'

'Was this an act of protest on behalf of child refugees around the world?'

'What was in the note?'

'Who put you up to this?'

'Where are you from? Were you born in this country?'

'Would you like to sell us your story?'

Everywhere we looked, there were lenses and lights and loud clicking sounds. I clung on to Josie and Michael and Tom as the one-eyed machines all pushed us into a circle. I could hear Josie's breathing beginning to wheeze – she doesn't like tight spaces – and my hands were beginning to sweat. Michael and me shouted 'NO COMMENT!', but I don't think anyone could hear us.

'EVERYOBODY STAND BACK RIGHT NOW!' came a cry. And just as suddenly as the scary cameras and reporters and microphones had surrounded us, they all instantly moved away, and we could breathe again.

'NO SHAME AT ALL!' shouted the same familiar voice, which was getting closer and closer to us. 'HOW DARE YOU HARRASS MY KIDS!'

We saw Mrs Sanders pushing past the cameras like a red-faced bull and reaching out her hand to us. 'STAY

OFF SCHOOL PROPERTY! AND IF I SEE **ANYONE** NEAR THESE KIDS AGAIN, I'LL BE CALLING THE POLICE **AND** THE QUEEN'S GUARDS!'

Grabbing my hand, Mrs Sanders stormed back in through the school gates pulling us like the trailing tail of a kite behind her. She stopped briefly in front of Mr Irons, who was now standing by the school doors. 'MR IRONS! YOU WERE SPECIFICALLY INSTRUCTED TO WAIT AND BRING THESE CHILDREN IN SAFELY. WHERE WERE YOU?'

Mr Irons gave us all a cold stare, his nose deadly quiet.

'I'm afraid I didn't see them,' he said, his eyes narrowing even more and his moustache getting twitchier.

'YOU DIDN'T *SEE* THEM! STAY HERE! I WILL SPEAK TO YOU LATER.'

Throwing open the school doors, Mrs Sanders led us in and stopped to look down at us properly. She was angrier than I had ever seen her and her whole face was the colour of an extra bright pink peach. 'Are you all OK?' she asked. Her voice was back to a normal volume now but it was shaky.

We all nodded, too stunned to say anything.

'Anyone hurt?'

We shook our heads.

'Good. Now all of you are to go straight upstairs to my office,' she ordered, looking over her glasses at us. 'You'll find Mrs Khan already there, along with Ahmet and his foster mum and Ms Hemsi – and two police officers who want to have a quick word. I'll be up in just a minute. I need a word with Mr Irons!' And waving us along, she hurried back outside.

I think there are two types of being scared in the world. The first type is when you do something wrong – like breaking your mum's favourite vase by accident, and you're scared of her finding out, but at the same time, because she's your mum, you know that deep down she won't ever punish you too horribly because she knows that accidents happen.

But then there's another type of scared. It's when something you never, ever thought would happen, suddenly does. And the idea of it is so awful that you want to run away. I've only ever felt this type of scared once before. And that was when I saw Mum standing in the hospital corridor crying, and I knew right away that something bad had happened to my dad.

I was feeling that second type of scared again now, and it made me want to be sick all over the floor. I had never thought that the Greatest Idea in the World would get us into trouble with the police. And I never ever imagined it would get Ahmet into trouble too. I didn't want him to feel angry at us. But what if he hated us for not telling him our plan – and for the news people knowing about him, even though we hadn't meant them to?

'Come on,' said Josie, putting an arm over my shoulder. And together, we all walked in silence up to Mrs Sanders' office. I took a deep breath and, fearing the worst, opened the door.

But instead of angry stares and shaking heads, we found everyone smiling at us. Mrs Khan ran up and gave us all a hug, and so did Ms Hemsi, and Ahmet looked at us with his wide lion eyes and gave us a small wave. His foster mum was holding her hands to her lips as if she was praying, and kept saying, 'You dear children!' And there were two police officers standing near the door, but they didn't look angry either and just nodded and smiled at us.

'Come and sit down,' said Mrs Khan, leading us to four chairs that had been squeezed in front of Mrs Sanders' desk.

We all sat down. I was still feeling jumpy inside, but at least I wasn't feeling sick any more.

'As soon as Mrs Sanders gets back, we want to hear all about what happened yesterday,' said Mrs Khan. 'Ms Hemsi will translate everything for Ahmet. And we want you to take your time, because it's all very important.'

'But Miss . . . what about first period?' whispered Michael, showing her his watch as it started flashing a blue colour. Just as he held it up, the bell for registration began to ring.

Mrs Khan smiled. 'Don't worry. Miss Stevens is taking the class this morning.'

We immediately felt sorry for everyone in class. Miss Stevens is learning to be a teacher, but she's so boring and always spends so much time writing on the board that everyone hopes she won't ever really become one.

Mrs Sanders came in, and, squeezing past everyone, sat down in her big chair that had a squashed green velvet pillow on it. 'Right!' she said, clapping her hands once. 'Begin!'

Slowly at first, and then getting faster and faster and faster, we began to talk. We talked about how we became friends with Ahmet and how we wanted to help after finding out about where his mum and dad might be. We talked about hearing that the border gates were going to be shut and about all the plans we had come up with to help. I could see Ms Hemsi explaining everything to Ahmet as we went, and his eyes getting wider and wider. But it wasn't until I got out my exercise book and showed everyone the Greatest Idea in the World and the Emergency Plan, that he jumped up from his seat and came to stand next to me. Ms Hemsi had to stand up too as we continued to talk about the letter to the Queen and the presents we were meant to give her, and Stan the Taxi Man, and Davinder the Paramedic, and the Extra-Extra Special Cold Stream Guards who had given us their word.

Nobody asked us any questions. Not even one. They all just sat and listened and nodded as Ms Hemsi murmured what we were saying in Ahmet's ear. It was strange having so many grown-ups sit and listen as if we were them and they were us, but it felt good too.

When we had said everything there was to say, Mrs Sanders nodded and put her hands together.

'Well,' she said, leaning back in her chair. 'I hardly know what to say.' She leaned forward and picked up my exercise book with the Greatest Idea in the World drawn in it. 'But what I *can* say is that Ahmet is very, *very* lucky to have friends who are so passionate about helping him find his family.'

Mrs Khan nodded, and I saw the two police officers nodding too.

'Now just to be clear,' said Mrs Sanders, peering over her glasses at us. 'What you did was extremely dangerous. And your plan – or the likes of it – must never, *ever*, be attempted again. Do you understand?'

We all nodded silently. I could feel my cheeks getting hot and saw Tom's ears instantly turn bright red.

'You lied to Mrs Khan, you left school without permission and you put yourselves in great danger. Behaviour like this would usually lead to a temporary suspension from school.'

Josie gasped and Michael winced. I could hear Tom swallowing nervously and even Ahmet looked scared.

Mrs Sanders went on. 'However. We've spoken with all your parents, and I can understand fully that you thought this was an emergency. So . . .'

I looked up at Mrs Sanders and could feel everyone doing the same.

'In this instance, you will not be suspended.'

Tom yelped a small 'Yessssss!' and Josie let out a huge puff of air that had been making her cheeks swell, and Michael gave a long sigh. And as soon as Ms Hemsi had told him what had happened, Ahmet cheered and clapped. But even though I felt happy too, I couldn't feel fully happy because I still wanted to know something.

'And what about Ahmet's family, Miss? Has the Queen found them already?'

Mrs Sanders shook her head and slowly leaned forward. 'I think you should all know that the Queen . . . well, there are some things that even she can't do.'

'But she's the *Queen*,' frowned Tom. 'She can do whatever she wants!'

I could see Ahmet staring at Mrs Sanders as if she wasn't making any sense to him either.

But Mrs Sanders was shaking her head. 'I'm afraid that's not quite true. I'm sure that the Queen would like to try and help Ahmet in some way, but I doubt very much that she'll be allowed to send out extra people to find his family. Especially when no one knows where they are.'

On hearing Mrs Sanders' words, I felt something hard hit me in the middle of my chest. I wanted to tell her that she was wrong – that the Queen could help anyone if she really wanted to. But even though my mouth opened, it couldn't say any words.

'I know that may come as a huge disappointment,' said Mrs Sanders, peering over her glasses at us and looking at me the longest. 'But Ahmet has lots of people trying to help him find his parents. Though even if they do find them, it may take a long time – months, maybe even years – before they can join him here. That's why he's staying with Ms York for now,' she added, nodding at Ahmet's foster mum.

We all stayed silent. And even though I didn't want them to, I could feel my eyes beginning to get wet and my nose tickling and something heavy sinking in the pit of my stomach.

Everything we had done had been for nothing. And the Greatest Idea in the World was really the Stupidest Idea in the World. In fact, it was probably the Stupidest Idea in the Whole Universe! And I knew that everyone was thinking it too.

'Now,' said Mrs Sanders kindly. 'I want to show you something.' She took a newspaper from out of her bag and laid it on the desk in front of us.

I looked over at Michael and Tom and Josie, but I think they must have all forgotten about the promise we made, because they immediately started to read the paper. So I wiped my eyes and looked at it too. I knew that it had to be OK to break a promise to your mum if your head teacher was telling you to.

A huge headline stared up at us from the front page, and, alongside it, was a large blurry image of me running up to one of the Queen's Guards with Tom behind me. I could tell it was me because of my bright blue rucksack, but I couldn't see my face properly at all.

The paper looked like this:

The story said that the newspaper was going to run an international appeal to find Ahmet's parents, which made Josie grin and whisper 'See?'

This is what it said:

Yesterday afternoon saw a centuries-old tradition in disarray, when the Changing of the Guard ceremony was disrupted by two nine-year-old children. Breaking through the barriers, they attempted to give one of Her Majesty's palace guards a written note, asking the Queen to help them find the family of a refugee boy known only as 'Ahmet'.

The decisive actions of these children have served to remind us all of the shameful hesitancy and fear which often govern our actions – and those of our government.

So, who is Ahmet, and where is his family?

This paper is determined to help, and urges our readers, our leaders and our politicians to do what they can to not only find this young boy's missing family, but reunite them here on UK soil.

Perhaps it is the actions of these children which will inspire political bodies across the world to finally heed the plight of refugee children everywhere. A fitting testament indeed, to a young boy – whose story we have yet to learn – made infamous by a daring act of true friendship. We appeal to all of you to not let the brave actions of these children be in vain. Help us find Ahmet's family!

After she had finished, Mrs Khan put the paper down and looked at us with her eyebrows raised. 'So, you see . . .' she said, clasping her hands together and placing them under her chin, 'all is not lost. Even if the Queen can't do as much as she'd like to, there is a whole world of people who are whispering Ahmet's name and trying to think of how to help instead.'

Later that morning, as I sat in lessons, I thought about what Mrs Sanders had said. I thought about the World Wide Whispers being whispered right at that very moment, and wondered how long it would take for all of them to reach the border gate people – and Ahmet's mum and dad too.

I had never thought about how loud a whisper can be if there are lots and lots of them. So, all that day, I whispered 'Help Ahmet' out loud too, whenever I could. So did Tom and Michael and Josie. And whenever we did it together, our whispers made us sound like an ocean.

23

BRENDAN-THE-BULLY AND THE BREAKING NEWS

There are some days that you never, ever want to forget. Like birthdays and school trip days and adventure days.

And there are other days when you want to forget everything that ever happened. Like when a bully bullies you, or a grown-up tells you off for doing something you didn't do, or when someone you love most in the world suddenly dies.

And then there are Rollercoaster Days. Those are days when one moment you're so happy that you feel like it's your birthday, but then the next you feel so sad that you want to hide in your bed until everything is over.

That Friday, the day after we had learnt about the World Wide Whispers, was a Rollercoaster Day.

After the morning register, Mrs Khan suddenly told everyone to leave their things on their desks because we had to go to an emergency school assembly. We only ever have an emergency assembly if something bad has happened – like a fight or if something's been stolen from a teacher. But Josie clapped her hands and asked, 'Do you think they've found Ahmet's parents already?'

That made my heart leap up and feel like it was flying – maybe the emergency assembly *was* for that! So I looked over at Ahmet and gave him an excited wave.

But the assembly wasn't for that at all. Mrs Sanders only wanted to tell everyone to be on their best behaviour – even the teachers – because the reporters surrounding the school were clearly 'not going anywhere any time soon' and had put the school 'firmly on the world's radar'. Hearing this made everyone sit up straight, just in case there was giant radar being beamed down from outer space to spy on us.

Then Mrs Sanders said that if anyone spoke to a reporter about me or Tom or Ahmet, or asked us any questions about what had happened, the police would know, and they might be expelled. This made everyone turn around and stare at us and I could hear Jennie saying loudly, 'See! Told you it was true! They did break into the Queen's house!' and someone else reply, 'They should have worn a mask! Then they wouldn't have been caught!' But we didn't mind – and Josie and Tom even started acting like famous people and began waving at everyone.

But as we were leaving the assembly hall, Brendan-the-Bully pushed past us and whispered, 'Smelly Refuge Bag!' at Ahmet, and Chris and Liam punched their fists into their hands which meant they were going to beat us up.

I thought we should tell Mrs Khan and Mrs Sanders right away, but Ahmet told me not to. He said bullies that just talk are better than bullies that actually punch because words don't hurt as much. I don't agree. Dad always used to say that words can hurt more than punches, because when you get a bruise or a bump after being punched, it disappears after a while and you can forget all about it. But words can stick around for a long time, and the meanest words stick around the longest.

Tom didn't think Ahmet was right either and said we should pull down Brendan-the-Bully's pants in P.E.

Josie thought we should save up all our pocket money and pay one of the bigger bullies to bully him for us. But then Michael said that bullying a bully was silly, and that we should just ignore him. So that's what we all agreed to do.

Except we couldn't.

Because at first break, Brendan-the-Bully started to do something which made me hate him more than anything I had ever hated in my whole life. Even beetroot and Mr Irons. Mrs Khan says we should never, ever hate anyone because hating someone can eat up your insides and gives you heart disease. But sometimes you can't help it. And I especially couldn't help it when I heard Brendan-the-Bully and Liam and Chris singing the song they had made up.

The song went like this:

> *Ahmet the refugee smells like poo!*
> *So we're gonna stuff him in a bag,*
> *And flush him down the loo!*

I got so angry that as soon as I heard it, I shouted at them to shut up and leave Ahmet alone, and so did

Michael and Josie and Tom. But that only made them sing it louder and louder and louder, which made Ahmet's face get redder and redder.

I looked around for a teacher to tell, but Mr Irons was the only teacher I could see on duty, and I could see right away that he had heard Brendan-the-Bully's song too and wasn't going to do anything about it. He just stood and watched us with his nose in the air.

By the time Brendan-the-Bully had begun to sing the song for the fourth time, I think all of us had forgotten what Mrs Sanders had said about everyone being on their best behaviour and the giant radar and about there being lots of reporters everywhere. Because suddenly, without even thinking about it, I made a running lunge for Brendan-the-Bully – and Tom and Josie and Michael did the same! We all crashed into each other and, falling to the floor, began punching and kicking Brendan-the-Bully and Liam and Chris just as hard as we could. I think I must have been punched and kicked back too, but I was so angry I couldn't feel anything.

Ahmet stood frozen to floor and watched us, not knowing what to do, but after a few seconds, he roared and, jumping on top of Brendan-the-Bully, began to hit him as hard as he could too!

The fight didn't last for more than a minute, because a few seconds after we had all fallen to the floor, we could hear a whistle hurrying our way and clicking noises like camera buttons being pressed, as lots of pairs of hands started to pull us away. We were marched into school and up the stairs and the next thing I knew, we were all standing in Mrs Sanders' office, being stared at angrily by not only Mrs Sanders, but Mrs Khan and Ms Hemsi too.

I couldn't really hear what they were saying because my ears had become so hot, but I think I heard the words, 'ashamed', 'never in the history of the school' and 'parents' being said. We all got a detention for fighting – even Ahmet. But it wasn't all bad. When my ears had cooled down, Josie told me that when Mrs Sanders had heard Brendan-the-Bully's song, she had given him and Liam and Chris two weeks' detention, and said she would be calling their parents too!

But as it turned out, Brendan-the-Bully's punishment was more serious than even we could have imagined, because by that very evening, Brendan-the-Bully – and Mr Irons – were Breaking the News.

On every single channel, and in all the weekend papers, headlines like 'Video of Bully Attacking Refugee Boy Sparks Outrage', and 'Teacher Stands Aside as School Bully Threatens Refugee Boy' and 'School Bully Trash-Talks Refugee Child' were everywhere, so that by Monday morning, the school was surrounded by even more cameras and reporters and vans with satellite dishes on their roofs than before.

Brendan-the-Bully and Liam and Chris didn't come into school for three whole days after they had broken the news, and when they did, their parents came with them and made them apologise to Ahmet in front of everyone at morning assembly. They still had to do detention every day for two weeks too! It made everyone glad they had been caught by the news people.

Brendan-the-Bully still looked at Ahmet with a horrible scowl on his face whenever he thought no one could see him, and one time in the lunch hall, he walked up right up to Ahmet with his fists clenched as if he wanted to punch him. But instead of being scared, Ahmet just looked at him with his lion eyes and grinned.

After that, Brendan-the-Bully never went near Ahmet again.

And just when we thought things couldn't get any better, that week Mr Irons and his whistling nose disappeared too and were never heard of ever again. Boring Miss Stevens had to take over his class, which probably made them just as miserable as they had been before. But no one else really cared about that, because now everyone was free to scream and laugh and shout as much as they wanted to at break-times again.

So we did – except we all screamed and laughed and shouted louder and longer and harder than we had ever done before.

Because when you're playing with your friends and don't have any bullies to worry about any more, that's exactly what you should be doing.

THE INTERVIEW

Although Brendan-the-Bully wasn't bullying Ahmet any more and Mr Irons was gone, I was still feeling worried. Eight whole days had passed since our Emergency Adventure and Ahmet's parents still hadn't been found. And even though Mrs Sanders had said the Queen couldn't really help us, I knew that deep down we were all still hoping she would do something.

The hardest thing was trying to make Ahmet understand that the Queen hadn't been able to help. Every morning, as soon as he would see us in the playground, he would ask, 'The Queen will find today, yes?'

After a few days of trying to tell him 'No' and seeing him look sad, we began to shrug and say, 'Maybe' as hopefully as we could.

'The gates will have been shut last Friday,' said Josie quietly, as she gave her ponytail an angry pull. Even though we didn't usually have P.E. on Thursdays, Mrs Khan had decided to treat us, so we were all sitting on a bench waiting for the climbing frame and feeling sad.

'Ahmet, your turn,' said Tom, pointing to the free space at the climbing frame.

Ahmet ran over to the bars and leapt up to the highest rung he could reach. He was as good at climbing as he was at football. When I asked him how he could jump so high and climb so fast, he shrugged and said, 'Fences'.

'If the gates are shut already and no one's helping us to find Ahmet's family, why do you think the reporters are still here?' asked Michael, carefully patting the sides of his Afro so that it would stay in place when it was his turn at the climbing frame.

It was a question all of us had been asking ourselves, because even though there were fewer reporters than last week, they were all still asking us questions about Ahmet whenever they saw us.

'Maybe they think we'll try and do something else to help Ahmet find his family and they're just waiting to see what it is?' suggested Josie.

For the rest of the day, we tried our best not to think about the reporters and the newspaper appeal and the Queen, but on the way back home, a reporter suddenly shouted out, 'Kids! What do you think of Mr Fry's views about refugee children like Ahmet?' and another one shouted, 'Do you have a response? Do you want to say something back to him?'

We all said, 'No comment', just like we always did, but we gave each other a puzzled look. None of us knew who Mr Fry was, or what he had to do with us or Ahmet, but we promised each other we would try and find out that night.

When I got home that afternoon, I found lots more reporters in front of my flat. It was strange because there used to be only one or two before – but now there were at least fifty and they were all shouting questions at me about Mr Fry! I ran past all of them just as fast as I could and saw Mum standing just inside the main door looking out for me.

'Mum!' I cried out, running up and hugging her as she quickly buzzed the door open. 'You're home early!'

Mum hugged me back and hurried me inside. When we got to our flat, I could see the television was on, which was another sign that something odd was happening, because Mum only really watches telly at night.

Quickly switching off the telly, Mum bent down to look at me closely and asked, 'Are you OK? It can be scary having so many people chasing you and asking questions.'

I nodded. 'But, Mum, why are you home early?'

Mum stroked my cheek before replying, 'Because I need you to do something *really* important – and help us all to help Ahmet.'

Motioning for me to sit down at the kitchen table, Mum placed a large peanut butter sandwich in front of me and a glass of milk. My stomach gave a growl because it likes peanut butter sandwiches the best. Even though they make my mouth go sticky.

'Darling, do you know who Mr Fry is? He came to your school once – a long time ago. He's our local MP.'

I frowned and shook my head. 'But the reporters were asking about him.'

Mum nodded. 'I bet they were,' she said, shaking her head as she sat down opposite me. Grabbing some newspapers from the kitchen counter, she spread them out in front of me. 'This is why,' she said. Her voice was calm but her cheeks were pink so I could tell she was cross about something.

I looked down at the newspapers. They were all different, but all of them had the same picture on the front page. It was of a man with grey hair wearing a dark suit and a blue tie, and above him in big letters were headlines like, 'No More! Refugee Influx Flooding Britain' and 'Britain's Needs Must Come First' and 'MP Fry labels Buckingham Palace Kids "Radical Refugee Terrorists"'.

My heart beat fast at the last headline, but before I could read anything else, Mum gathered the papers back up again.

'Let's put these aside for now, darling. I don't want you to read the articles because most of it's just silly nonsense.' I watched as Mum turned to put the newspapers back onto the counter and then faced me again. 'The reason I showed them to you is because I wanted you to see the kinds of headlines Mr Fry has helped to create today, and for you to understand that there are some people – like him – who think refugee children like Ahmet shouldn't be allowed into the country.'

'But why not, Mum?' I asked, feeling angry. 'They haven't done anything wrong!'

'I know that – and I'm sure deep down, they know that too. But remember what we said about some people being afraid of anyone different to them?'

'So you mean Mr Fry – and all the people like him – are just like Mr Greggs?' I asked, scrunching up my nose as if the name smelled.

'Yes, exactly,' grinned Mum. After a few seconds the grin disappeared. 'And there's also something else you need to know. Mr Fry, you see, has said it was *Ahmet* who made you and Tom go to Buckingham Palace that day and—'

'But that's a lie!' I cried out, feeling my cheeks beginning to burn.

'I know it is, darling – and so do lots of other people. But that's why I've had a long talk on the phone with Mrs Sanders and . . . Well, we've come up with a plan.'

I sat up and, pushing my sandwich plate away, told my ears to listen extra carefully – because any plan of my mum's would be the best plan ever!

'Now. We think that people like Mr Fry shouldn't be on the front pages of *any* newspaper. It's *your* story, and Ahmet's story that people need to hear. So, how would you feel about talking to a reporter today – and telling them all about your letter to the Queen and Ahmet trying to find his family, and all the things that you've done for each other?'

'But – you told me to say "no comment" . . .'

'I know I did,' said Mum. 'I wanted to protect you, and Ahmet too. But when people like Mr Fry start telling lies, it's time to speak out.'

'So you mean I should tell them about the Greatest Idea in the World and the Emergency Plan and the Queen and *everything*?' I asked, feeling both scared and excited.

'Yes,' said Mum. 'But it won't just be you on your own. Tom and Josie and Michael and Ahmet will be with you too, and you can all share your story together.'

I clapped my hands. 'Mum, that's the BEST plan in the whole world!'

Mum laughed and, getting up, said 'I'm glad you think so! Now finish that sandwich and let's get back to school! Mrs Sanders has suggested we hold the interview in your classroom, so we need to be there in . . .' Mum looked at her watch. 'Half an hour. Plenty of time for you to wash your face, and look your best too. Chop-chop!'

I gobbled down my peanut butter sandwich, gulped down my glass of milk, scrubbed my face, brushed my hair, polished my school shoes, and, checking I had the Greatest Idea in the World with me in my rucksack, got Mum to tie my school tie extra neatly. I thought I had done everything in three minutes, but then Mum said, 'That was good for ten minutes!' which made me look at the clock and shake my head at it.

As we headed downstairs to the main door, Mum grabbed my hand and said, 'We're going to have to run very fast to the bus stop, OK? Let's pretend all the journalists are zombies out to get us!'

I nodded and grabbed Mum's hand tightly. I tried to tell my heart to stop thumping so loudly because there weren't really any zombies around, but it wouldn't listen. As soon as Mum opened the door, I ran just as fast as I could, pulling Mum behind me. I heard her say 'In a rush! No comment!' until we reached the bus stop.

When we got to school and walked into our classroom, Tom and Michael and Josie were already there with their parents, and Ahmet was with his foster mum and Ms Hemsi too. Mrs Khan was talking to two people I had never seen before, but Michael told us that one was a lawyer and the other one was a Case Worker.

'What do you think they're all talking about?' asked Josie, looking at the grown-ups standing in the corner and whispering.

'Probably about that horrible MP who's saying Ahmet made us go to Buckingham Palace,' I said.

'Really?' asked Josie. 'Mum and Dad didn't tell me anything about that! They just said if I helped tell the story we'd get some money for a proper holiday.'

Just then, Mrs Sanders walked in, followed by a woman in a suit and a man with a camera.

'It's them,' whispered Josie loudly. 'The reporters!'

'Everyone,' said Mrs Sanders, waving them forward. 'This is Ms Hall and Mr Myers.'

We looked up at Ms Hall and Mr Myers, who smiled and waved at us.

'And this is Ahmet's caseworker, Mrs Khalid,' said Mrs Khan, pointing at the woman in the glasses standing next to Michael's mum.

We all smiled.

'Let's begin, shall we?' clapped Mrs Sanders. 'First, Ms Hall is going to speak to the four of you about the Greatest Idea in the World. And then she's going to speak to Ahmet – with Ms Hemsi's help, of course. And Mr Myers will be filming you all and then will take some nice pictures of the plans. Have you got them?'

'Right here,' said Mum, holding up my rucksack.

After Mrs Sanders and everyone had finished fussing over our hair and collars and jumpers and ties, we all sat in a row and The Interview began.

It only lasted ten minutes, but it felt much, much longer. Ms Hall asked us what made Ahmet so special and why we had wanted to help him. It was hard answering more than one question at the same time – especially with so many grown-ups and a large camera staring at us. But Tom said it was because Ahmet was the only boy he had ever met who had seen real bombs and guns and had been fast enough to run away from them; and Michael said anyone who had walked millions of miles to come to school deserved to be helped; and Josie said that Ahmet was the best footballer she had ever seen – even better than her – and that it wasn't fair that he didn't know where his parents were;

and I said that Ahmet was the bravest person I had ever met, because even though he had run away from a real-life War and found it hard to speak English and missed his family all the time, he was still the best kind of friend anyone could have.

After that, Ms Hall asked us about the Greatest Idea in the World and the Emergency Plan, so we showed her and the camera the drawings and talked about how we had gone to the Queen for help because we thought she could do anything.

'And are you disappointed that the Queen hasn't contacted you?' asked Ms Hall.

We all nodded.

'What would you say to her if you could – in fact, what would you say to everyone out there listening to you today?' asked Ms Hall.

'That the gates need to be kept open!' said Tom without hesitating.

'Yeah,' said Michael. 'They should be kept open for everyone like Ahmet.'

'And everyone needs to help Ahmet find his parents,' said Josie. 'Because it's not their fault they've gone missing!'

Ms Hall nodded and, looking at me, waited for an answer.

I wanted to say lots and lots of things to the Queen and the Prime Minister. But instead I said, 'I er ... I think ... We should all help anyone who's a refugee – just like my Grandma Jo did ...'

I heard Mum gasp as Ms Hall leant forward. 'Your Grandma Jo helped refugees too?' she asked, looking interested.

I nodded. 'In the World War – the second one.'

'And how did she help them?' asked Ms Hall, gently.

I looked over at Mum, who nodded at me, her eyes wide and watery. 'She ran away from the Nazi people and then she helped other people run away from them too.'

Ms Hall cleared her throat and, giving me a smile, turned to Ahmet to ask him about all the things he had seen and what he had run away from.

I watched as Ms Hemsi helped him translate what he wanted to say into English, but I liked his last answer the best. Because when Ms Hall asked him how he felt about what we had done, he looked at us and without any help, said, 'I happy to have best friends on planet.' And just like that, I knew the answer to my very last question.

When we got home that night, Mum tucked me into bed and said she was proud of me, and that wherever Dad and Grandma Jo were, they were very proud of me too.

'In fact, I think if Grandma Jo were alive today, she'd give you a big fat kiss, and tell you exactly what she told your dad when he was your age,' said Mum, stroking my hair.

'What was that, Mum?'

'That the entire world is full of hearts searching for a place to call home. But refugees are different, because they don't just look for a home. They look for peace too. And because of that, they possess the most special hearts anyone could ever have.'

Hearing about what my Grandma Jo had said to my dad made me so happy that I couldn't sleep for a really long time. Not until I heard an owl hooting from somewhere very far away.

The next morning, I woke up extra early and jumped out of bed. I thought Mum might still be asleep, but she was sitting at the kitchen table drinking tea.

And, in front of her, was a newspaper.

'Morning!' she said, smiling as her mug of tea steamed up her glasses. 'Thought I'd run out and get the paper. Look . . .' She held it out to me.

Staring back at me, from the front page, was a picture of me and Tom and Josie and Michael, all sitting in a row. Tom and me were holding up the Greatest Idea in the World and Josie and Michael were holding up the Emergency Plan. Next to it was an even bigger picture of Ahmet, smiling. And above all our heads in big bold letters, were the words:

AHMET: THE MOST FAMOUS REFUGEE BOY IN THE WORLD

EXCLUSIVE: THE CHILDREN BEHIND THE BUCKINGHAM PALACE PROTEST

'Come over here, you,' said Mum, opening her arms 'Let's read it together, shall we? School isn't for another two hours, so we have lots of time . . .'

Squeezing onto Mum's chair, I read the article with her. It ran onto two whole pages, but I liked the bits where Ahmet was speaking the best. He spoke about his family and where they might be, and how he dreamed of being a footballer one day. But he also spoke about his sister being in the sea, and how hard it was being bullied and having horrible songs being sung about him.

'I hope that shuts up all the other bullies too!' muttered Mum angrily, when she read that bit.

'Mum, look!' I cried, as we turned over the page to read the second half of the article. 'There's you!'

I leaned forward to see the picture better. Mum was standing next to Tom's parents and Michael's parents and Josie's parents and Ahmet's foster mum, and the words underneath said:

PARENTS UNITE TO FIGHT AGAINST RACISM & CHAMPION REFUGEE RIGHTS

'Racists like MP Fry have no right to tear innocent families apart!'

'Mum?' I asked, after we finished reading the whole article.

'Hm?'

'Do you think the Queen and the Prime Minister and the border people will see this? Do you think they might all try and help now?'

Mum squeezed me tight. 'I don't know, darling. But what I do know is that by us sharing our story, lots more people will be talking about it. And that has to be a good thing.'

I put my hands down on the newspaper and then had another thought.

'And do you think it might make people like Mr Fry and Mr Greggs be less scared of Ahmet?'

'I'm not sure,' said Mum, smiling. 'But when it comes to people, you just never know!'

I didn't know about Mr Fry or Mr Greggs, but on the way to school that day, Josie said that after her mum and dad had listened to Ahmet's story, they had told her she had been right to make friends with him.

And that made me have a Thought.

Maybe it didn't matter if *really* horrible people like Mr Fry or Mr Greggs didn't like Ahmet. Maybe they didn't even deserve to know him. But people like Josie's mum and dad did, because they weren't horrible at all. They had just been nervous about making a new friend.

THE QUEEN'S MESSAGE

I thought we were pretty famous before the interview, but I was wrong.

It was only after we became 'Headline News' that I found out what being famous was really like. Wherever we went, Tom and Michael and Josie and Ahmet and me were waved at and smiled at and patted on the head and given thumbs-ups by lots of people we didn't know. People at the bus stop and on the streets would run up to us and say things like, 'God bless you!' and, 'We're all behind you, Ahmet!' and, 'I just signed the petition! Parliament's gonna listen to us! You'll see!'

Even Mr Banik, who owned the newsagent's near the school bus stop and was famous for hating children, ran out whenever he saw us and gave us each a chocolate egg. For free. And not just for a day, but for a whole week!

But as exciting as it was to be famous and to be friends with the Most Famous Refugee Boy in the World, what happened a few days later was even more surprising.

On Wednesday morning, just six days after we had done The Interview, we arrived at school ready to play football, but couldn't find Ahmet anywhere in the playground. When the bell began to ring we headed straight to class. But when we got to our classroom, he wasn't there either. Neither was Ms Hemsi.

'He's probably just late,' shrugged Josie, as we sat down. But Ahmet was never, ever late. I looked over at Mrs Khan and wondered if I should ask her. She was busy getting the class to sit down, but she looked happier and couldn't stop smiling, even when she was telling Clarissa off for being late.

After registration, Mrs Khan said that Mrs Borneville was going to take first period today as she had something to do. Then she came over to me and Josie and Michael and Tom and told us to come with her.

'Are we in trouble?' whispered Tom, as we followed Mrs Khan down the corridor.

'But we haven't done anything ... have we?' whispered Josie.

I didn't say anything; me and Michael just looked at each other.

Mrs Khan knocked on Mrs Sanders' door and waited for a 'Come in!' before she pushed it open.

The first person we saw was Ahmet. He was perched on a chair, his face looking surprised and serious and happy all in one go. Sitting on one side of him was Ms Hemsi, whose cheeks were pinker than I had ever seen them, and on the other, were two men. They each gave me a wide smile. For a moment I couldn't remember how I knew them, and then Tom gave a gasp. 'It's the Queen's Guards!' he cried out, punching me on the arm.

He was right! They really were the Queen's Guards! Except they were dressed in suits and didn't look so giant because they weren't wearing their tall black hats!

As we walked in, they stood up and gave us a salute. Josie squealed in delight and Michael was so excited he shook hands with both of them at the same time.

I looked over at Ahmet, who, on seeing that we knew the Guards, was now smiling at them fully.

'Come in, come in,' said Mrs Sanders, waving us to our seats and peering over her glasses at us.

'Children, these gentlemen have a very special message to give to you,' said Mrs Sanders.

'We certainly do,' said Lieutenant Kungu. 'It gives me great pleasure to present you with this very special message from the Her Majesty, the Queen . . .' He took an envelope from the inside of his coat and held it up.

'And seeing as how The Greatest Idea in the World was your idea, how about *you* open this?' he asked, as he held the envelope out to me. It was large and square and cream and had the curliest writing on it that I ever saw.

As I took it, everyone crowded around me to stare at it.

I turned it over. On the back was a large blob of red candle wax. It looked like it had been spilt accidentally, but there was a 'EIIR' stamped in the middle of it, so it must have been done on purpose.

'Go on,' whispered Josie, and Ahmet and Michael and Tom nodded. I carefully peeled off the wax blob and pulled out the letter. The writing was so curly and scratchy and I was so nervous that I couldn't read the words. Seeing me struggle, Mrs Khan came and stood behind me. I gave her the letter so that she could read it out loud instead.

This is what it said:

Dearest children,

Lieutenant Chris Taylor and Second Lieutenant Walter Kungu were so kind as to inform me of your brave – although slightly dangerous! – actions undertaken on behalf of your refugee friend, Ahmet. I have now also received the letter you had written to me on the subject beforehand. Thank you for the very colourful envelope and the lovely stamps. Purple is quite my favourite colour!

I was very sorry to hear of Ahmet's plight – I have heard of many little boys and girls like him. Thanks to your brave actions, lots of people from all over the world are working together to try and locate his family. I know they will all be trying their very best, and I look forward to hearing of their safe arrival to the United Kingdom (or Queendom as you so nicely put it!) soon.

My Lieutenants tell me that you had brought tea and biscuits and gifts in the hopes of sharing them with me. That was a lovely idea!

I am unfortunately scheduled to go on a small tour across Britain this week, but when I get back in a fortnight's time, I should like nothing better than to invite you all to have tea with me at the palace.

Until then, I must ask that you please do not go running after any more of my soldiers. It was awfully dangerous, and I am most relieved that you were not hurt. Any letter addressed to me will always reach me and I do like to receive mail – especially one so beautifully decorated and written with such care.

With my fondest best wishes,

Elizabeth R

(92 years old)

After Mrs Khan had read it out loud for us and Ms Hemsi had finished telling Ahmet what the letter said, we all sat in silence. I guess there are just some things that even grown-ups don't have any words for – and a message from the Queen is one of them.

THE PRESENT

It's been two weeks since we were all in the newspapers and received the Queen's letter and, in lots of ways, things feel just like they did before. Mum doesn't walk me to the bus stop any more, and strangers have stopped staring at us with funny looks on their faces, and I'm still hoping to win first prize for my photosynthesis plant, even though Ahmet's plant is growing faster than everyone else's again. He's teaching me some words in Kurdish like 'grow more' and 'grow up' and 'I love you lots', and I think it's working!

But in lots of other ways, things aren't normal at all. Aunt Christina comes round much more often and she buys me presents too. I think she likes us now because we were in the newspapers. I still don't like her. Whenever she comes, I ignore her and make Uncle Lenny play Scrabble with me and Mum like he used to do.

Mr and Mrs Rashid from the floor below have invited Mum and me for dinner this weekend which means Mum might have a new best friend.

And next week, I'll be going with Tom and Josie and Michael and Ahmet to Buckingham Palace to have tea with the Queen. Sometimes I get so excited thinking about it that I have to jump up and down just as high as I can until my insides feel calmer. I think they must know that things can never be the same again after you've had tea with an actual Queen.

Mum asked me what I'd like to take as a present for the Queen and I thought about it for three hours. In the end, I decided that, as she doesn't really need anything, and I can't afford to buy her real diamonds or a ruby, I would buy her a pomegranate from the man with the royal heart. Because I think the next best thing to wearing lots of jewels must be to eat lots of little ones instead.

The other thing that's changing is that I turn ten today. When I woke up extra, extra early this morning, I found the Birthday Card on the kitchen table.

The Birthday Card is a very old card. It was the last one Dad gave to me before he died and, every year, Mum puts it out so that he can be there to greet me when I wake up, just like he used to when he was alive.

It doesn't say much inside. Just:

To my Pumpkin,
HAPPY BIRTHDAY! Try not to grow up too fast!
Love, Dad X

I'm glad Mum had to leave for work early, because seeing the card always makes me want to sit down and cry. So, I did. And then I went to my room and played one of Dad's favourite songs on his old record player. That made me feel better too. Sometimes all you really need is somewhere to cry without anyone ever knowing.

I didn't remind anyone it was my birthday because I wasn't having a party and I didn't have anything to take into class with me. Josie brings in a big cake on her birthday and Michael's mum always hands out goodie bags to everyone. But Mum doesn't have time to bake and goodie bags are expensive. That's why it's easier to pretend that I don't have a birthday at all.

I met Tom and Josie and Michael by the bus stop as usual, and when they didn't say anything about my birthday, I felt sad and glad at the same time. I was afraid Mrs Khan might say something, but she didn't. My Uncle Lenny usually sends me something in the post, so I would probably get home to find a card with some extra pocket money or chocolate in it like I did last year. If I did, that would be nice.

At afternoon break, Josie and Tom and Michael and Ahmet and me talked about what we were going to wear to Buckingham Palace next week. Josie's mum was going to buy her a new dress and a new pair of football trainers. Michael was wearing a suit with a bow tie. Tom said he had a purple suit his uncle had made him wear to a wedding in San Francisco but which might not fit any more. And Ahmet said his foster mum was going to buy him something at the weekend, and that he would also take his rucksack.

'You can't take your rucksack with you,' said Josie. 'It's old and ripped and it's got a hole in the front pocket! The Queen might not even let it inside the palace.'

'But important!' said Ahmet, looking panicked. 'My dad give me for birthday before war – and I carry from Syria, so next time I see, I tell him it is seen by Queen!'

'Oh,' said Josie, looking sorry that she had said anything.

'Then you have to take it,' I said. 'The Queen will want to see it.'

'Yeah,' said Tom. 'And your dad will love it.'

Ahmet smiled and said, 'I know you to understand.'

The bell for last period began to ring, but as we all headed back to class, we met Ms Hemsi in the corridor outside. She was clasping her hands together and her eyes looked red. As soon as she saw us, she ran over and, whispering something into Ahmet's ear, took him by the hand and quickly led him away.

'Where's she taking him?' asked Josie, as Ahmet looked over his shoulder with a confused look on his face.

None of us could think of an answer, so we made our way into class. After we had all got out our spelling books and had spent ten minutes learning the meaning and spelling of three new words – 'possession', 'depression' and 'objection', there was a light knock on the door.

We all looked around to see who it was. After a few seconds, Ms Hemsi's head popped around the door, and after giving Mrs Khan a thumbs-up, disappeared again.

Mrs Khan smiled and, clapping her hands, said, 'Right, everyone! Close your books please. I have a very important announcement to make.'

We all fell quiet and waited for an explanation about what was going on – and where Ahmet was.

'Today is a very special day,' said Mrs Khan. 'And we have a few very special guests to help us celebrate.'

Everyone turned around to see if there was anyone at the door, but there was no one there yet.

'Eyes to the front please,' ordered Mrs Khan. 'Now, before our guests arrive, I want you all to promise me that you'll be on your very best behaviour!'

Everyone shouted, 'We promise, Mrs Khaaaaaan,' wondering who the guests could be.

'Do you think it's the Queen?' whispered Josie.

'Maybe it's the Queen's Guards again!' whispered Tom.

But they were both wrong, because it was my mum! Carrying a cake with candles on it! And behind her was

Mrs Sanders and Ahmet's foster mum and Ms Hemsi and the woman who had been at The Interview and who Michael had said was Ahmet's Case Worker, and another woman we'd never seen before who was walking with her hand on Ahmet's shoulder. I could tell Ahmet was happy because he was smiling, but his eyes looked wet and a little red too – just like Ms Hemsi's had in the corridor.

And within a few seconds, the whole class was singing 'Happy Birthday' to me just as loudly as they could.

After Mum helped me blow out the candles, Ahmet and Ms Hemsi and the woman who still had her hand on his shoulder stood at the front of the class with Mrs Khan.

'Quieten down please, everyone!' called out Mrs Khan. 'We'll cut the cake in just a few minutes, but first, I want everyone to say "Good afternoon" to our extra-special guest, Ms Duncan.'

The woman standing beside Ahmet stepped forward as everyone shouted out, 'Good afternoon, Ms Duncaaaaaan!' She was wearing a bright blue suit and had short grey hair and a green diamond ring.

'Now. Ms Duncan has come here today from very far away, because she has some important news to share with us all,' said Mrs Khan. 'Over to you, Ms Duncan.'

Ms Duncan nodded and looked straight at me with a smile before looking around at everyone.

'Good afternoon, everyone. I'm from the Home Office, which is a government department that controls who comes in and out of our country.'

'Like the police?' called out Dean.

'No, not like the police,' smiled Ms Duncan. She waited for more questions but no one else said anything.

Everyone was deathly silent now, and I could feel my whole chest beating so hard that it felt like someone was playing drums inside my tummy.

Ms Duncan carried on. 'Today, I had the pleasure of bringing Ahmet some special news. And he has very kindly said that he would like to share it with all of you. Ahmet?'

She held out a plain white envelope that had no address on it, and offered it to him.

But Ahmet didn't take it, and whispered something to Ms Hemsi instead.

Ms Hemsi frowned at first, but then laughing and crying all at once, gestured at me to come up. 'He would like his best friend to read it to everyone,' she explained.

For a moment, I couldn't move. Then Josie gave me a kick under the table that made me stand up and slowly walk over to where Ahmet was standing.

Ms Duncan waited until I was standing in front of her and, holding out the envelope to me, said, 'A very happy birthday, Alexa, from all of us. Thanks to you – and to Josie and Michael and Tom of course – there have been thousands of people writing in and signing petitions and calling our offices, just to ask how they could help Ahmet and lots of other refugee children like him. And because of that . . . well . . . here you go . . .'

Ahmet nodded and added, 'Happy birthday, best friend.'

I opened my mouth, but I think all my words must have disappeared and my brain had stopped working, because I couldn't really think any thoughts any more.

Ahmet tapped the envelope in my hand, and said, 'You read it! For me . . .'

I tried to take the piece of paper out of the envelope, but there were so many eyes staring at me and Ahmet's

293

eyes looked so big that my fingers got nervous and started to shake.

'Here, darling . . . let me help,' whispered my mum, as she jumped up and quickly took out the folded piece of paper that lay inside. Opening it up, she held me close as we read it out loud together. It said:

STATUS – FAMILY INVESTIGATION SUMMARY:
AHMET SAQQAL (AGED 9)

FATHER: MOHAMED SAQQAL
AGE: 43
PROFESSION: PROF. OF ENGINEERING
COUNTRY OF ORIGIN: SYRIA
STATUS: *LOCATED*

                                 CALAIS REFUGEE CAMP, FRANCE

MOTHER: SAMIRA SAQQAL
AGE: 45
PROFESSION: JOURNALIST
COUNTRY OF ORIGIN: SYRIA
STATUS: *LOCATED*

                                 MED FAC. SURUC, TURKEY

SISTER:	SYRAH SAQQAL
AGE:	3
STATUS:	DECEASED, MED. CROSSING

H.O. OUTCOME: GRANTED PERMANENT ASYLUM IN THE UK. REUNIFICATION OF FAMILY IMMINENT.

I looked up at Mum and then at Ahmet and then back at Mum again.

'What's as-as-asylum mean?'

My mum smiled but her eyes were watery too. 'It means they can come and live here, darling . . . Ahmet's mum and dad are coming to the UK! They've been found!'

I looked up at Ahmet, who was nodding excitedly.

And then I looked up at Josie and Tom and Michael, who were all staring back at me with their mouths open.

And then I looked at Mrs Khan, who was saying a prayer and Ms Hemsi, who was crying so much that she had grabbed Mrs Sanders and was making her go red in the face.

And suddenly Michael jumped up and shouted, 'WE DID IT!' and the whole class started cheering and whooping and jumping and clapping all at once.

I know that afternoon was one of the best afternoons I will ever have. Not because it was my birthday, but because it was an end to one of the best adventures a brand new ten-year-old could ever have, and the beginning of a whole set of new adventures that I bet even Tintin never had!

And it was all thanks to a boy who came and sat at the back of the class, and who let me be his friend.

A SPECIAL THANK YOU TO ALL THE CHILDREN (AND THE EXTRA-NICE GROWN-UPS) WHO HAVE READ THIS BOOK

Did you know that by reading and whispering lots about this book, you will be helping refugee children and their families receive some very precious gifts?

That's because the author will gift a portion of all the royalties* she receives to some wonderfully brave people who spend every single day trying to help save and rebuild the lives of refugees all over the world.

So whether that's food and water, warm clothes, shelter – or lots and lots of chocolate to help make their insides feel happier, thank you for each and every gift you will be helping deliver to refugee children just like Ahmet, and their surviving families.

* In case you were wondering just how royal the author's 'royalties' will be, we're very disappointed to inform you that it doesn't include any gifts from the royal family or the Queen! In fact, 'royalties' is just a very grand term to describe whatever money the author will be making from the sale of each book. But then again, if you really, really think about it, as every coin and note printed in the UK *always* has a picture of The Most Royal Person in the Land, every penny and pound really is quite royal . . . Perhaps that's where the term 'royalty' comes from! (Maybe you can look the history of the word up yourself and let us know if we're wrong . . .)

DID YOU KNOW?

There are currently over 65 million refugees trying to flee
ongoing wars, man-made environmental disasters,
economic destitution or political persecution.

That's more than the total number of refugees who fled
Nazi persecution during World War II (UNHCR, 2016).

Described as 'the biggest refugee and displacement crisis
of our time' by the United Nations Secretary-General
Ban Ki-moon, the ongoing wars in Syria, Yemen, Iraq,
Afghanistan, Sudan (and many more), mean an increasing
number of people are trying to find a safe home
elsewhere.

7 QUESTIONS TO HAVE A DEEP THOUGHT ABOUT (WITHOUT GIVING YOURSELF A HEAD ACHE . . .)

1. Have you ever met a Refugee Kid?
If you have, have they ever told you their story?
If you haven't, how would you try and help them if you did?
If you are yourself a refugee child, what is the hardest thing about meeting new people?

2. If you had to run away from a war and leave your house and school behind forever, what three things would you take with you?

3. Most refugee children have to learn a brand new language very quickly after leaving their country, and find it very difficult to get used to the sounds and the way everyone around them is speaking. If you had to go to another country where no-one could speak your language, what would you like people to do to help you understand them better?

4. Have you ever read any newspaper stories about refugees or heard grown-ups speaking about them? What words did they use to describe refugees, and how did they make you feel?

5. If you could give a Refugee Kid one gift to help make them feel happy, what would it be?

6. What do you think should be done to help stop the refugee crisis – and who would you ask to help?

7. And finally, if you could be famous and on the news for a single day, what action would it be for?

WHAT'S IN A WORD?

The word 'refugee' has a very special meaning, and is different to the word 'immigrant'.

An 'immigrant' or 'migrant' is someone who has deliberately moved to a new country (immigrant) or another part of their home country (migrant) because it is what they wanted to do – it was their choice. There are lots of reasons why people want to move to a new part of the world. They may want to live in a nicer house (like Dena's parents) or somewhere with more trees, they may have found a brand new job, or they may simply want to be closer to people they love.

But a 'refugee' is not an 'immigrant' or a 'migrant', because they have been forced to leave their homes and countries suddenly, and risk a chance of death if they do not do so. According to international law, it is legal to leave your country to try and find safety in another country – and to travel as far as you need to until you find a home.

PIECES OF YOUR OWN PUZZLE

I was born in . . .

My parents come from . . .

My most favourite thing to eat is . . .

If I could travel anywhere in the solar system, I would go to . . .

If I was visiting the Queen, I would wear . . .

My best friend in the Whole Wide World is . . .

The thing I'm best at doing is . . .

In my family, the funniest person is . . .

When I grow up, I want to be just like . . .

WORLD WIDE WHISPERS

Contrary to the whispers you may have heard,
the UK has taken in less than 1% of the world's refugees.

In fact, it is mostly countries *outside* Europe that look after
4 out of 5 of the world's refugees.

Can you guess which ones?

Turkey, Lebanon, Pakistan and Ethiopia each take care of
millions of refugees, and between them, outweigh the
numbers of refugees taken in by all the 50 countries of Europe
combined.

AUTHOR'S NOTE

Up until September 2015, I had never really thought about what the words 'refugee crisis' really meant. Even though it was something that was being spoken of by the news every day, it felt like an invisible crisis – something that was happening in countries far, far away and to people I knew almost nothing about.

But at 11am on 2nd September 2015, that all changed. Not just for me, but as I later came to find out, for thousands of people across the world. Because that was the morning nearly every single newspaper around the globe broke the story of Alan Kurdi, a young boy who had died at the age of three, trying to cross the Aegean Sea with his family.

Reading that story filled me with a series of endless questions. How had this been allowed to happen? Why had I not done something sooner? And what could I do now? Because I knew I had to do something – no matter how tiny that something might be.

Those questions spurred me into action. I hunted down agencies that were working to save refugees' lives and raised what donations I could for them, and after a while, I decided to visit the closest refugee camps I could find, and deliver aid directly. I began to venture out to the refugee camps of Calais whenever I could.

Ahmet's silent strength is a testament to the many young children I have had the honour of meeting in the forests, broken tents, muddy plains or huts and makeshift shelters in Calais and Dunkirk. Even after having survived horrors and cruelties, each child's capacity to be cheeky, to laugh, to find joy or instil it in others is a gift I will always remain in awe of.

From the many faces of those beautiful children, I have dedicated this book to Raehan, 'the Baby of Calais': a baby of only a few weeks old, whose mother had survived the destruction of her village, and a journey of thousands of miles whilst pregnant. Following the demolition of the official campsite at Calais, baby Raehan and his family disappeared, and I can't help hoping every day that they made it safe and sound to the family members they had in the UK.

Until then, the legacies of Alan Kurdi and baby Raehan go on through the work of the thousands of kind hearts who help refugees to not only survive, but find safety and a home they can call their own again.

ACKNOWLEDGEMENTS

Thanking every person who has been part of this incredible whirlwind of a journey is going to be harder than writing and editing the book combined! Simply because it has taken an army of amazing hearts to get me here. So here goes . . .

First and foremost, for putting up with all the manic parts of me, for nursing me through two surgeries and a decade of pain, for running out and getting me enough chocolate and favourite foods and the medicines I needed to keep me going, and for never giving up on me even when I had given up on myself, my love and eternal thanks to my beautiful mum, Salma Shirin Raúf, and my brother Zakariah. (Zak, you once commented that I'd probably have died of stupidity and starvation if it hadn't been for you both. I didn't have a response, because we both know you were right!)

To my agent / silent defender, Silvia Molteni, who

took me on even though I submitted my first manuscript with a covering letter that began with 'Dear Dear', my endless gratitude for your calm perseverance, and for planting the seedling that led to this book. I'll never forget the moment you phoned to tell me this was happening, and am still in shock you made it all so. There aren't enough words.

To Lena McCauley, my editor and the most patient human being on the face of this tiny planet called Earth, thank you for bearing with my consistent ability to disappear abroad when stressed, record-breaking computer crashes and endless yo-yo-ing. You have made this book so much more than what it was, and I owe you a lifetime of spa treatments (as a minimum!). My trust in you is bone-deep, and there is no-one I can imagine who could have handled this book better.

To the Orion Children's Books family, headed for me by the equally itchy-of-foot, Helen Thomas, thank you all for welcoming me so warmly as you have done. My especial love and thanks to Dominic Kingston for being as passionate about handwritten letters, vellum paper and wax seals as me, and for seeming to spend most waking hours PR-ing this book, even when he has fifty others to contend with too!

To Pippa Curnick, thank you for getting the drawings so spot on it's scary, and my copy-editor 'Lady Genevieve Herr' (as I call you in my mind) for your honesty and fearless questioning.

I am, I believe, one of the luckiest souls in the world, enriched as I am daily by souls infinitely wiser, kinder and far worthier than my own. To the real Selma Avci, thank you for believing in my writing since Day Zero (nearly two decades ago!), and for loving all my stories no matter how bad they were and continue to be! I hope you and Turgay Ozcän never stop reading or laughing. Ever. Even if what you're laughing at has to be me!

Remona Aly, in the last ten years that I have been blessed with your friendship, my universe has expanded in ways unfathomable. Thank you for every memory made, the endless prayers gifted and for your unshakeable faith in me. I'm so glad we got pretend-married in Ireland!

To the sharer of my literary dreams, Sughra Ahmed, and kindred-spirit-cousin, Piya Muqit, thank you for encouraging me, sitting with me through the dark times, and giving me the loving kicks I needed to get this book done.

To Caroline C. Cotett, the personification of calm amidst the storm, and co-founder of the Women's Refugee Centre (WRC) Dunkirk: I feel so honoured to have met you and will be eternally grateful to Timothy Gee and the Quakers In Britain for that blessing. I can't wait to go on working with you to help the refugees you give your all to, every hour of every day.

To my first and eternal refugee aid convoy team:

Dahlia Basar (panini-sandwich maker supreme); Atif Butt (le Capitan!); Homaira Sofia Khan and the unstoppable Yasmin Ishaq; and every volunteer or team member who has ever gone out with me to Calais and Dunkirk: thank you for always saying 'Er . . . ok' even when you thought I was mad, for the endless fundraising, goods-raising, cooking, packing, loading, shopping, and being brave enough to drive on the wrong side of the road. I would never have embarked on this journey without you all. Especial love to Khola Hassan and the Ilford Women's Islamic group; Taiba Shah; Anoushka Khan; Yasir Mirza, my Nurun Khala and every dear heart who has gone on donating and supporting me and my teams whenever the call for help is made.

To my general welfare and sanity team: Ayisha Malik, authoress supreme for (a) being the reason why I approached PFD and Silvia in the first place and (b) calming me down when I thought I couldn't hack the ride; Satdeep Grewal and Alex Thomas for your quiet faith in my writings and wicked sense of humour; Jacquelyn Shreeves-Lee for reading the first draft of the book with such joy; Nadia Abouayoub for writing with me in the early days in the Wallace Collection before you found your falcons and began to disappear to the Highlands; Sumiya Hemsi for your heart, laughter and loving Mum almost as much as I do; Batool for the passionate care you impart; Yasmeen Akhtar for your elegant, Audrey Hepburn-esque wisdom; Asha Abdillahi; Rabia Barkatulla; Shaista Chisty; Sajeda Qureshi and Mockbul 'Mycroft' Ali; Julie Siddiqi and countless other hearts who keep me inspired and laughing. You know who you all are.

To John Crawford (my beloved step-in dad), and Victoria Dyke, thank you for reading this in its first draft (inclusive of some blindingly bad drawings) and getting me to sign the copy, thinking it was worth your time to do both those things. I love you both endlessly.

To all my nieces and nephews: Inara, whose gurgling kept me going during that first draft; Kamilah, whose gorgeous eager-to-befriend heart always makes me smile; Zahir, whose questions about the Second World War were an inspiration (and not tiring to answer at all!); cheeky Eshan; and my other two hearts, Kasheefa and Maeesha, thank you for making my world so utterly joyous.

To every refugee forced to search for peace so far away from the place they once called home: there is more love for you than you can imagine. Go on. The peace will come.

And as the umbrella to all the above, my heart lies in thanks at the feet of God. For heeding my prayers, making this happen, allowing me to live on, and telling me 'not yet' when I needed to hear it most.

Photo © Rehan Jamil

Onjali Q. Raúf is the author of *The Boy At the Back of the Class*, *The Star Outside My Window*, the World Book Day title *The Day We Met the Queen*, *The Night Bus Hero*, *The Lion Above the Door*, *The Great (Food) Bank Heist*, *Hope on the Horizon* and the upcoming fairy tale collection, *Where Magic Grows*. She is also the founder of O's Refugee Aid Team, an organisation which seeks to raise goods, funds and awareness to help refugees access all the forms of help they need. You can find the aid team on Twitter @o_refugee.

When she's not writing or working on behalf of her NGOs, she can be found with her head buried in a book at the local bookshop. You can find Onjali on Twitter @OnjaliRauf.